*"I couldn't get you
out of my mind.
I had to see you again."*

His eyes ran down her, appreciating the way the shiny fabric molded itself to her moist body and lingering on a bead of water trembling in the cleft of her breasts.

"Why the sudden change?" she demanded. "What do you want?" Her heart flailed at her ribs like a frantic sparrow.

"You." His mouth came down over hers, and the heat of his hands, moving slowly and soothingly on her back, made her feel as if she were wearing nothing at all.

"Forget the train," he murmured against her mouth. "Stay with me. I'm only asking for a day."

250

Dear Reader:

After more than one year of publication, SECOND CHANCE AT LOVE has a lot to celebrate. Not only has it become firmly established as a major line of paperback romances, but response from our readers also continues to be warm and enthusiastic. Your letters keep pouring in—and we love receiving them. We're getting to know you—your likes and dislikes—and want to assure you that your contribution does make a difference.

As we work hard to offer you better and better SECOND CHANCE AT LOVE romances, we're especially gratified to hear that you, the reader, are rating us higher and higher. After all, our success depends on *you*. We're pleased that you enjoy our books and that you appreciate the extra effort our writers and staff put into them. Thanks for spreading the good word about SECOND CHANCE AT LOVE and for giving us your loyal support. Please keep your suggestions and comments coming!

With warm wishes,

Ellen Edwards

Ellen Edwards
SECOND CHANCE AT LOVE
The Berkley/Jove Publishing Group
200 Madison Avenue
New York, NY 10016

STORMY PASSAGE
LAUREL BLAKE

SECOND CHANCE AT LOVE
BOOK

Second Chance at Love books are published by
The Berkley/Jove Publishing Group
200 Madison Avenue, New York, NY 10016

For Michael

chapter 1

THE FAMOUS NATHAN TRENT was late. Ashley took another sip of Chablis and glanced first at her watch, then across the room to the only empty table in the restaurant. It stood in a coveted corner spot, just below an oil painting of dahlias glowing darkly in a copper bowl, and it was reserved for the man whom Clayton Pridemore, with a touch of jealousy, had once called His Majesty, Nathan Trent.

"Would Mademoiselle care to order lunch now?" the waiter at her elbow inquired for the second time.

"Not just yet," Ashley said in uncertain French, and pretended to study the menu again. Clay had told her that the elusive Trent lunched at one o'clock every Saturday at the same restaurant, a few blocks from his home on the Rue de la Jeunesse. But Clay had not seen Trent in years. Perhaps he had changed his habits.

Just then she noticed the restaurant proprietor leaving his post and hurrying toward the entrance, his face wreathed in smiles.

The instant she saw the man, framed in the arched doorway of the dining room, she knew it was he, though she couldn't say why. The woman at the next table, an attractive brunette who had been hovering over her salad with the delicacy of a butterfly, paused to look as well.

Perhaps it was his height. He was what people back home called a long, cool drink of water, and he carried himself so that every inch showed off to full advantage. Perhaps it was his air of assurance. Some people enter a room looking as though they own it. Nathan Trent looked as though he didn't care who owned it. Lean and fit, with mirthful blue eyes and a shock of black hair falling over his forehead, he stood chatting easily with the proprietor as his gaze wandered over the diners. Although he looked too rugged to worry about the finer points of fashion, his charcoal-gray suit was impeccably tailored and he had taken the extra bit of care necessary to arrange his tie in a Windsor knot. In Ashley's experience, such a detail characterized the perfectionist. She realized that she had expected him to be older. He was perhaps thirty-three to her twenty-six, but no more. Nathan Trent: owner of the chain of newspapers to which the *Chronicle* belonged, heir to the Trent publishing fortune. Ashley had been hearing of him ever since her student days at Creighton University in University Park, Pennsylvania, the school the Trents had endowed with so much money, but this was her first view of him. As his glance grazed her face, she flinched, but he was turning toward his table and appeared not to notice.

To hide her sudden nervousness, Ashley signaled for the waiter and ordered an omelette and a salad. By the time she had done so, Trent was occupied with his menu. She was able to observe him as she pondered exactly how to breach his well-known defenses and secure an interview with him. When she had first conceived the idea, back home in the offices of the *Chronicle,* she had intended to rely on her charm, which had always served her well before. But now, having traveled across the Atlantic to Marseilles and having hunted out the lair of the lion, she was no longer sure that would be enough. In spite of his present good humor, he was an awesome figure who looked as if he did not suffer fools gladly.

A pair of steady blue eyes met hers across the crowded

room, and she realized too late that she had been staring. She quickly assumed her most studious expression and tried to look as though she had been examining the painting just above Trent's head. Fortunately a party of departing diners came between them, giving her time to compose herself. But a moment later she saw that Trent, still looking her way, was speaking with a waiter. When the waiter approached her table, panic soared in her like a Roman candle.

"Mademoiselle," the waiter said in French, "the gentleman in the far corner, whose name is Monsieur Nathan Trent, presents his compliments to you. He is anxious to make your acquaintance and asks if you would be kind enough to dine with him."

Ashley's first thought was that she had misunderstood, armed as she was for her adventure with only basic French and less Italian. But Nathan Trent was still watching her, with the faintest of smiles playing about his mouth. For an instant only the feminine instinct to retreat tussled with the reporter's determination to advance. The latter won out. She could not help feeling flattered that he had singled her out, and she thought to herself that this was going to be easier than she had dared to dream. Whoever said that Nathan Trent was unapproachable? She smiled to herself as she imagined Clay's amazement and, she hoped, grudging admiration, when the newspaper received her interview with the great Trent.

"Thank you," she said to the waiter as she rose. "I accept his invitation with pleasure." She was glad she had worn the pearls and the simple cream linen dress, which set off her tan and the highlights in her honey-blond hair. Being at her best made it easier to face that Mediterranean blue gaze, which seemed to bore right through her.

Nathan Trent stood and pulled out a chair for her with a flourish that had more than a hint of irony in it. "It's a favorite of mine too," he said, indicating the painting with a nod. "I thought you'd like to see it up close."

"Thank you. It's lovely," Ashley said warily. "Better than the usual restaurant art."

His eyebrows shot up. "Oh, and are you an art expert, Miss—?"

"Forrester. Ashley Forrester. No, going to galleries is just a hobby of mine. I'm no expert."

"Well, I am, Miss Forrester. And I own that painting." He refilled his wine glass from the half bottle of Châteauneuf-du-Pape at his elbow and leaned back complacently. "I come here every week because the food is superb and the owner is a friend of mine. Since I come so often, why should I put up with restaurant art, as you call it, when I can substitute something more to my taste?"

"You're absolutely right," Ashley agreed, impressed that he would take the trouble. The touch of the perfectionist again. She was just beginning to relax a little, when Trent leaned forward and said in a more deliberate tone, "I come here every week, Miss Forrester, and I've never seen you before. I'm curious about that, since this little gem is one of the best-kept secrets in Marseilles. It's not on the tourist circuit. How did you learn of its existence?"

"A friend told me." She toyed with the stem of her glass. Things were not going according to plan. He was controlling the conversation, not she.

"A friend? Someone who dines here regularly? Perhaps I know him—or her." He was studying her carefully, his head to one side. "But if the friend likes the restaurant, why are you here alone?"

"He . . . couldn't come."

"No? That's a shame. You don't mind dining alone? Many women dislike it."

"You certainly ask a lot of questions," Ashley said with a trace of annoyance. "I almost feel—"

"—as if you're being interviewed?"

She nearly stopped breathing. However, Trent's expression gave no hint that he was suspicious. On impulse she decided not to tell him that she was a reporter at all, not at this meeting. The trick was to make sure he would want to see her again. Yet she seemed to hear an alarm ringing somewhere in her mind. It had been almost too easy to make contact with him.

As the waiter unobtrusively served them, she said, "I have a question too. You spoke to me in English right away. How did you know I wasn't French?"

"It's your walk. American women take longer steps and swing their shoulders more than European women do." He raised his glass. *"Bon appetit."*

For the moment she decided simply to enjoy the meal, although it was not easy with such a formidable personage seated across the small table from her. Nathan Trent dwarfed his surroundings. He was not handsome in the conventional sense, for it appeared that at some distant time his nose had been broken and badly set, lending a raffish touch to what would otherwise have been an aristocratic face. There were hard lines around his full mouth and sparks of silver among his dark, unruly locks. Money had not completely protected him, she thought. He'd fought his share of battles with the world, giving as good as he got.

He broke in upon her speculations. "Is this your first trip to Europe?"

"Yes, it is," she allowed.

"Are you here as a tourist or on business?"

"I'm on vacation," she replied, a half truth at best, for it was a working vacation.

"And what do you do for a living?"

Ashley hesitated and averted her eyes from his. "Actually, I'm sort of between jobs right now." Which, again, was partly true. She had already made up her mind to resign from the *Chronicle,* and the series of travel articles she was to do about the Riviera—her real reason for being in Europe—were to be her ticket to a new life, to a job on the staff of a travel magazine far away from Clayton Pridemore, editor of the *Chronicle* and the man she had almost married.

"Tell me, Mr. Trent," Ashley said in some desperation, wishing to deflect his questions, "what do *you* do for a living?"

"Oh, come now, Miss Forrester." Trent folded his napkin and laid it beside his plate. "You know what I do for a living."

Ashley froze.

"Who do you work for?" he snapped. "A magazine? A newspaper?"

She swallowed, feeling more foolish than she had ever felt in her life, but she managed an insouciant laugh. "Is it so obvious?"

"It takes one to know one, *cherie.* I'm an old reporter myself."

"Then you knew from the beginning. You asked me to your table only to make a fool out of me!" Ashley flared, as the cruelty of his invitation began to sink in.

"I didn't make a fool out of you. You did that all by yourself," Trent observed dryly. "A very amateurish move, Miss Forrester, trying to catch me unawares on my day off, like some Peeping Tom photographer."

"I am not an amateur," Ashley shot back. "Don't you dare say that to me."

"Then tell me your qualifications."

She started to rise, then sank back in her chair. Somehow she wanted very much to prove herself to this man. "I got my journalism degree from Creighton University," she said, meeting his gaze straight on, "at the Andrew C. Trent School of Journalism—"

Trent threw back his head and let out a whoop of laughter. "Grandfather would have enjoyed you. He liked spirited females."

"I went to work at the *Chronicle,* in University Park, after graduation. I started out covering women's clubs and teas, but I'm a feature writer now. Last month I did one of the big weekend spreads."

"The *Chronicle?* One of my own papers? So, a viper in my bosom," said Trent sardonically. "And you have no other experience?"

"I don't plan to stay at the *Chronicle* forever," Ashley said grimly and added to herself, not after what happened with Clay.

"Of course you know the editor, Clay Pridemore," said Trent, as if he were reading her thoughts.

Hearing the name Pridemore aloud sent a chill over her, for it had almost been her name. "Yes," she said shortly.

"Clay's a good newspaperman. I picked him to head up the *Chronicle* myself. But personally . . . well, there's no love lost between us," Trent remarked cryptically. "The last I heard he was going to marry some precocious cub reporter on his staff. How did that work out?"

"I had no idea you took such an interest in the personal lives of your underlings," Ashley said too sharply. "The *Chronicle* is a very small part of your organization."

"I take an interest in everything that concerns Trent Enterprises," he said, continuing to stare at her boldly. "Is this Clay's idea of a joke, sending you over here to ambush me?"

"Clay knows nothing about it!" Ashley exclaimed so forcefully that Nathan Trent sat back in surprise.

"Well, well. I have the feeling there is more to this than meets the eye. Are you really all on your own, Miss Forrester? Don't tell me you came all the way to Europe for this little conversation."

"No," Ashley said. "I'm here to write a series of travel articles. This was not part of the assignment."

"Then accosting me was your own idea? Get a scoop and earn a promotion? Pick me up in a restaurant—"

"You invited *me* to join *you,*" Ashley cut in, enraged.

"But it was you who were staring, making yourself conspicuous, trying to conceal your true purpose—ah, well, enough." Trent made some small sign and the waiter materialized before them. "Put all of this on my account, Pierre. And see that Mademoiselle has whatever else she would like." He pushed back his chair and stood, towering over her. "Let me tell you a thing or two, Miss Forrester. My dislike of publicity is well-known. Better people than you have tried to get an interview with me, without success. But if you must try these games, please improve your technique. As you may have noticed, it is I who have interviewed you, and not the reverse."

Picking up Ashley's hand, he turned it over and kissed the palm. "It's been amusing."

He sauntered out, chuckling to himself and leaving Ashley blushing to the roots of her hair, staring down at her tingling palm, and despising Nathan Trent.

chapter 2

"WHAT HAS IT been like working for Nathan Trent?" Ashley asked. "Tell me from the beginning."

Charles LeSueur, a former classmate at Creighton University, leaned back in his chair and steepled his fingers under his chin. "You're really going ahead with this story, after what you say happened at the restaurant two days ago?"

"Well, I can't do a first-person interview without his cooperation," Ashley admitted, "so I haven't decided what to do. But he made me so furious, Charles!"

"And being furious made you curious."

"I suppose so." Trent's superior smile flashed before her eyes and she shifted impatiently in her chair. "Besides, I don't like to give up on something I've started. I'm not a quitter."

"All right," Charles said. "But—" he held up a finger "—this has to be confidential. No quoting me. I'd like to keep my head on my shoulders."

"All right."

Charles lit another cigarette. "What has it been like working for him? It's been a thorough education in journalism, and I have to say that I've been treated well. So if you're looking for criticism of him, I can't give it to you. Here I am, barely into my career, and I have an excellent position at the *Mediterranean Report*, the brightest jewel in the crown of Trent Enterprises. I came aboard the day after I graduated and have been promoted steadily ever since. Of course," he added with a smile, "it hasn't been easy. I've worked harder and put in longer hours than I ever thought possible. I've had to, to come up with the quality Trent wants. He's a hard man to please." At the ring of the telephone, he broke off. "Excuse me."

While Charles was occupied with some editorial question, Ashley strolled to the window and looked out over the slate roofs and chimneys of the old part of Marseilles. Gulls wheeled in the distance and the breeze was heavy with the salt tang of the sea. It was good to see Charles again. Blond and dapper, he had scarcely changed in appearance since they had studied together a few years before. Nor had he changed in personality. He was still a cheerful, nonthreatening sort of man—unlike some she could name—who never made any demands beyond friendship. The only thing that bothered her about their reunion was that it was taking place in the editorial offices where she knew Nathan Trent spent most of his time.

"You remember how the Trent interviewers used to come to campus looking for fresh talent," Charles resumed, replacing the receiver in its cradle. "Why didn't you try for one of the overseas jobs? I knew you wanted to travel, so I was surprised to hear you'd stayed on in University Park."

Ashley sighed and went back to her seat. "It's the oldest story in the world. I took a temporary job with the local paper. Then I fell in love. When that happened, I forgot everything else—my career plans, my desire to see the world. Six months ago I was engaged to be married to the editor of the *Chronicle*. The week before the wedding I discovered . . ." she faltered, disliking the idea of criticizing anyone, even Clay. "Let's just say that Clay's ideas on marriage turned out to be quite different from my own. He wanted a wide-open arrangement, one that would allow him to continue living as he always had."

"You mean, to continue relationships with other women?"

Ashley winced. "Yes. And silly me, I believed in true love and in being faithful to each other. He told me I was pathetically old-fashioned."

"There's nothing wrong with that," Charles said blandly. Ashley knew that he could not really imagine the cost of a broken love affair. Charles was simply not the emotional type.

"Perhaps not," she agreed, "but anyway I gave too much of myself to a lost cause. 'All for love and the world well lost'—that's me." She smiled ruefully. "I won't be so hasty next time."

"At least you're willing to allow a 'next time' to happen," Charles pointed out.

"Yes, I'm not permanently embittered. Just very careful. And my career comes first now." Ashley waved a hand. "I don't really want to talk about that. Tell me more about your employer."

"Really, there's probably not a lot that you don't already know," Charles reflected. "He's the third generation of the family publishing dynasty but not one of the idle rich. That was his decision, apparently. He took care to learn the business from the ground up, getting on-the-job training at every level—as a stringer for the AP, copy editing and even, literally, studying the nuts and bolts. If something goes wrong with the actual printing machinery somewhere, they say he can roll up his sleeves and fix it. An extraordinary man, in his way. His family originally had ties in the area where you and I went to school, but he was an only son and is all alone now. He's lived in Europe ever since he founded the *Report*."

Charles held up a paperbound volume and Ashley saw that it was the latest issue of the prestigious journal. "He writes a monthly column on political and economic issues, which has enormous influence."

"What about his personal life?" Ashley asked, genuinely captivated by the portrait that was beginning to form.

"I don't know. If he has any secrets, they're exactly that—secret. He's a very private person. I've never seen him outside the office. The general consensus is that his work is his whole life, though once in a while you hear rumors about his womanizing. But after—"

There was a sharp rap at the door just before it burst open. Nathan Trent strode up to Charles's desk, carrying a loose sheaf of papers. A pair of horn-rimmed glasses rode on the battered nose. His cuffs were turned back and his hair was tousled, suggesting a habit of running his hands through it while he worked.

"You'll have to revise this piece on Algeria," he told Charles. "We've just gotten a bulletin that changes everything. Let me show you." Suddenly aware of the other presence in the room, he wheeled sharply about. "Good morning, Miss Forrester," he said testily. "I thought we'd seen the last of each other."

"So did I," Ashley returned pleasantly, for she had made up her mind before coming not to be cowed by Trent, should they run into each other. She smoothed out the skirt of her softly gathered orchid dress, the one that made her blue-violet eyes shade toward violet, and waited.

"So, Charles, has she been pumping you for her exposé on me?" he asked, taking in the note pad and pen in Ashley's lap.

Before Charles could answer, Ashley volunteered,

"Charles is an old friend. We went to school together."

"It's a small world," said Nathan sarcastically, tapping the papers against his thigh with impatience. But then, as their gazes locked, Ashley felt something pass between them—a jolt of heat, energy, electricity. It was as if she had received a tiny spark of his being. In that moment, she decided on a gamble.

"I've given up my idea of writing about you, Mr. Trent," she said, replacing her note pad in her purse and standing up. "I only came to see Charles for a few minutes." She held out her hand and Charles rose to take it across his desk. "It's been great talking over old times, Charlie. When I get home, I'll send you some of my work."

"Oh, uh, I'd like that," Charles fumbled, trying to fathom the reason for Ashley's sudden departure.

"What made you change your mind?"

Ashley turned to Trent, who had asked the question. "Your rudeness the other day for one thing, even though I may have deserved it. But principally, Mr. Trent, I just decided you weren't interesting enough to write about."

"Call me Nathan."

"Nathan. And since I have a number of other stories to write and since I'm leaving Marseilles tomorrow, you simply don't seem worth the trouble. Besides, I'm told you care for nothing but your work, and what interest would that have for the average reader?" She paused to catch her breath and braced herself for a cutting remark.

He was silent, making up his mind about something. "Are you free this evening, Charles?" he asked abruptly.

"I was thinking of asking Ashley to have dinner with me, if she has nothing planned," said Charles, with a meekness that was almost comical.

"And do you have anything planned, Miss Forrester?"

"I would love to have dinner with you, Charles," said Ashley, ignoring the hulking figure beside her.

"Good enough." Nathan's tone was friendly but final. "I'm having some guests for dinner tonight. I'd like the two of you to join us. About eight."

Astonished that her gamble had paid off so soon, Ashley looked to Charles for a cue. His face was an open book. Clearly he was thinking of nothing but the honor that his employer was bestowing on him. Round two to Miss Forrester, Ashley told herself.

"Then that's settled," Nathan decided, taking their silence for consent. He dropped the papers on Charles's desk. "Look over the bulletin and my comments while I see Miss Forrester to the elevator. Then I'll be back to discuss them. Mademoiselle?" He took her arm and guided her out the door.

"So you're leaving tomorrow," he said as they walked down the hall of offices. "Where to?"

"To Rome eventually, with stops along the way." Ashley stretched her stride to match his and glanced up at his impassive profile. His grip on her arm was a shade tighter than it needed to be, and she almost felt as if she were being escorted to a frontier, thus to be forcibly evicted from his domain. "I don't suppose you want me questioning your staff," she blurted out.

He looked down at her pleasantly. "Question away. But my staff is loyal to me and I doubt you would uncover any news. However, I understood you were on your way out."

"Yes," she replied, "I am." Mollified by his unexpected cordiality, she added, "It's nice of you to ask an inquiring reporter to dinner."

"Well, I would say it's a little like acquiring a pet tiger," he returned, the corners of his mouth turning up in the suggestion of a smile. "I'll just have to remember to use a short leash and to keep up my guard." They reached the elevator, which stood open, an attendant dozing on a stool within. As Ashley stepped inside, Nathan said, "I must confess, I'm looking forward to it, Miss Forrester."

She turned to face him, and again, as their eyes met, the spark passed between them. "Call me Ashley." She smiled. "I'm looking forward to it too."

"Until eight, then, Ashley."

The attendant pushed a button, the doors closed, and they started down. During the slow descent, Ashley leaned against the wall and closed her eyes. She was still smiling.

chapter 3

AT TWENTY PAST eight that evening, Charles pointed from the window of the taxi and said, "That's where we're going—number thirty-seven."

Ashley, her sense of adventure running high, looked down the block of gray stone town mansions, known as *hôtels,* built in the seventeenth century, to one that was distinguished by a pair of caryatids, statues of women serving as columns, flanking the front door and supporting a small balcony that jutted out over the steps. A heavy iron gate stood ajar in austere welcome. The windows were lit up on every floor and through one she spied the blaze of an opulent chandelier. She could imagine that wily nobleman Cardinal Richelieu living in such a place, or one of the warrior princes of Condé. It was clearly a man's dwelling.

"I feel as if we're about to enter the Emerald City of Oz," she said with a nervous laugh.

"Yes, and we may never see Kansas again," Charles joked back. He handed a bill to the burly, garlic-breathed driver and they stepped out on rain-freshened pavement.

An elderly gentleman in black opened the door and ushered them to the threshold of the chandeliered room, where some twenty people milled in conversation as they sipped cocktails. Ashley just had time to admire the glassy parquet floor, which reflected and multiplied the prismatic light from above, and to notice that the walls were lined with oil paintings, when Nathan detached himself from a group before the fireplace and came their way.

"Glad you could make it," he said hospitably to Charles, shaking hands. Then, turning to Ashley, his face lit up with approval at the upswept hairdo and the lacy Victorian-style dress, both of which she had chosen to accentuate the slimness of her neck and waist and the fragility of her bone structure.

"Lovely," he murmured, taking her lightly in his arms to kiss her on both cheeks in the French manner of greeting. But instead of the perfunctory kisses in the air she expected, his lips, warm and firm, brushed each cheek slowly, exploring her skin and leaving behind a track of fire. Her hands spread themselves convulsively on his back and she felt his hard muscles ripple under the velvet dinner jacket, felt the overpowering strength of his lean frame. She closed her eyes, wanting the roomful of people to disappear, wanting him to kiss her on the mouth.

A silky, petulant voice shattered the magic. "Darling, you haven't introduced me."

Dazed, Ashley pulled away. Charles was speaking to a gray-haired man with a monocle. No one was staring her way. The room was still there. For an instant she almost believed she had imagined the shared rush of feeling. Then she looked at Nathan and saw a hotness in his eyes, fading but still evident.

"Darling?" This time the voice had an edge to it.

The woman was tall and thin, nearly as tall as Nathan, so that when she slipped her arm around his waist and snuggled up to him, one dangling beaded earring brushed his shoulder and her copper helmet of hair shone next to his raven curls. Most of her height was in a pair of long, bronzed legs, which showed through a thigh-high slit in her backless black dress. Steadying herself on teetering heels by leaning into Nathan, she regarded Ashley and Charles boldly from beneath heavily fringed lashes. Ashley was immediately intimidated by her aggressive elegance and by the feline cunning in the widely set green eyes. Her own appearance seemed embarrassingly girlish by comparison.

"This is Renata," said Nathan, his composure intact once more. "You may have seen her charming face on the cover of *Marie-Claire* last month. She's come to the provinces to recover from the hectic pace of modeling in Paris."

"And when Nathan is the doctor," said Renata, looking directly at Ashley, "my convalescence can take a long time."

"Really?" Ashley said, catching the droll look Charles threw at her. She knew what he must be thinking—that Nathan Trent had a more active private life than his staff even suspected.

"Charles works at the *Report*," Nathan told Renata, "and Ashley is a visiting journalist from the States."

Renata was not interested. Tugging on Nathan's sleeve, she announced, "I've come to take you away. There's a crisis in the kitchen—something about the *gigot*—and Marius wants your advice." Her green eyes flashed at Ashley, sending the unmistakable message: *You see what my position is here,* and she began to draw him away.

"Then I must leave you to make your own introductions," Nathan told the two of them. "Charles, we have some good American bourbon, if you'd like." From a passing tray he lifted a chilled, long-stemmed glass. "And I think this will be just right for you," he said to Ashley with a twinkle of amusement. "It's cool and light and not too sweet. But pretty, very pretty." Before handing it to her, he held the glass up to the light so that the contents glowed like molten rubies.

"What is it?" She took a tentative sip. It was good and she sipped again.

"An aperitif called kir. Dry white wine with a soupçon of crème de cassis—"

"Marius is waiting." Renata pulled at him again, a pout on her bee-stung lips.

"Yes, of course." Nathan turned to go, but not before Ashley had seen a crease of annoyance spring out between his brows. As she watched him leave, she noticed for the first time the merest suggestion of a limp in his stride and wondered what sort of accident had marred his straight, strong body.

"Well!" exclaimed Charles. "Mademoiselle Renata seems to have her claws into the boss."

"Nobody could," Ashley declared.

"What's this? Are you the world authority on him now?" teased Charles.

"I—I just mean his skin is too thick for anybody's claws," Ashley stammered, trying to cover up her emotions. "What do you say we start circulating? I'll never have another chance like this to meet the crème de la crème."

They separated and Ashley set out without a qualm to acquaint herself with the elegant assemblage, for as a reporter she was used to introducing herself to strangers. Within ten minutes she had spoken with the editor of the largest daily in Marseilles, with the Tunisian consul, and with a woman who had successfully climbed the Himalayan peak Nanda Devi. She had never ever been in such sparkling company, she told herself as she strolled over to examine a small painting that had caught her eye. Nathan and Renata still had not returned. Re-

membering the woman's hostility to her, she doubted
that there had been a kitchen crisis at all. Renata simply
wanted Nathan to herself.

The painting was, as she had surmised, a small still
life of fruit and a plaster cupid by Cézanne. She was
standing transfixed before it, admiring the subdued colors
and the utter perfection of the composition, when she
heard voices through the open doorway next to her.

"You left the seating arrangements to me and I made
them!" Renata's voice was thick with anger. "I spent all
morning matching people's interests and balancing
everything, and now you just want to throw my list out
the window!"

"That was before I invited two extra guests. There
will have to be some rearranging to accommodate them.
I don't see that it matters much." These words were low
and clipped. Nathan was coldly in control.

"Doesn't matter? Who are these people, anyway?
Some unimportant employees of yours. They should be
put at a table for two, by themselves!"

"I've told you what the new seating arrangement will
be. Mr. LeSueur is to be added to your table. Miss
Forrester sits at my table, and Madame Aumont and
Doctor Bianca will be moved to the table with the sen-
ator."

"Mademoiselle Forrester can sit somewhere else. I
won't have this!" A heel hit the floor.

"You are not mistress of my house. You will have
whatever I say. Now go change the name cards, as I told
you before. Now!"

Two sets of sharp footsteps sounded in opposite directions.

Ashley wandered away from the door, thinking furiously. Renata might not be mistress of Nathan's house-

hold, but she was undoubtedly mistress of his bed and she was obviously jealous of Ashley. Could she be dismissed as an insecure, possessive woman, or did she simply know Nathan only too well? Could he be expected to run after every new face? Scattered comments that Clay had made came back to her, remarks she had paid little attention to at the time. A heartbreaker, Clay had said, but the women never learn. They find him—or at least his money—irresistible.

Well, I can resist you, Don Juan, Ashley vowed. Just try me and see.

During this time the elderly manservant had been drawing back the heavy drapes of brown velvet along the outside wall to reveal a row of tall French windows. Now he opened the central pair and announced, *"Messieurs et Mesdames, le dîner est servi sur la terrasse."*

"May I escort you to dinner, beautiful lady?" Ashley looked up into Nathan's burning blue eyes.

"You may," said Ashley carefully, as, in spite of her promise to herself, her whole body began to glow in response to his nearness. Linking her arm through his, she bowed her head so that he might not read the desire in her face.

Renata swept by them with a man on each arm and her nose in the air.

They came out under the stars, on a low stone terrace scattered with candlelit tables. Torches burned in iron sconces set at the corners of the surrounding parapet. Before them stretched a walled formal garden, with ancient cypresses standing like sentinels along a central corridor. Ashley breathed deeply and smelled lavender and thyme.

"My secret garden," Nathan said with a smile, following her gaze. "Do you like it?"

"Yes, it's impressive."

"At the far end there is a rose garden with a statue by Houdon," he said as he held her chair. "I'll show you later. No, it's too wet tonight. We'll save that for another time. Excuse me for a moment." He went off to check his guests, stopping at each table for a few words. Distractedly Ashley introduced herself to her table companions, two businessmen, a woman lawyer, and a woman portrait photographer famous for her imaginative posings of the Beautiful People. *Another time,* she kept hearing. *We'll save that for another time.* Had it been an idle turn of phrase or had he meant what he said?

"I've discovered something in your absence," she said with an impish grin as Nathan took his seat beside her and a light seafood bisque was placed before them.

"Oh, and what is that?"

She nodded at the others, who were already engaged in a noisy discussion of French politics. "You and I are the only ones at this table who speak English."

"Exactly. I planned it that way." His chuckle was boyish and self-satisfied. "And they're an opinionated lot, capable of arguing for hours. So, unless you speak French better than I think you do, you'll have to content yourself with me."

"Is this the interview I've been seeking?" she asked archly.

"Why don't we do a series of interviews?" he proposed smoothly. "Off the record. Tomorrow."

Caught off guard, she stammered, "I'm afraid that's impossible. You know I'm leaving tomorrow."

Under the table, Nathan's hand found hers and grasped it tightly. "Stay another day," he said in a low, easy voice, "and I'll change your opinion about me. I can be very interesting to know."

"You don't understand." Her mouth had gone dry. "I have to keep to a schedule. The lifestyle editor at the *Chronicle* expects to receive my stories on a certain time-table." She tried to pull away but his grip only strengthened. Her hand was held captive against his thigh.

"What would another day—and night—hurt?" His thumb stroked her palm. "And don't use little Charles as an excuse. Anyone can see there's nothing there."

"And Renata?"

"Renata is leaving for a booking in Naples."

"Stop. this," Ashley hissed, much too aware of him physically. "You're asking the wrong person. I don't joke about such things."

Nathan brought her hand from underneath the table to his lips. The hotness was in his eyes again. "I'm not joking either, my dear. I'm perfectly serious. Accept and you'll find out."

"I know you're serious about the invitation," Ashley argued doggedly. "That's not what I mean. I mean, I don't go in for casual affairs."

"What's the matter?" The laughter in his eyes mocked her. "You wanted to be pursued this morning. Wasn't that the idea behind saying, 'I've given up the idea of writing about you, Mr. Trent'? Playing hard to get, weren't you?"

"That was a professional tactic," Ashley informed him crisply. "There was nothing personal about it."

"Then let's get personal."

Spellbound, she stared at him. In the flickering torch-light, his high cheekbones and gleaming teeth looked almost savage. "Why are you doing this?" she asked slowly.

"Because," said Nathan, "I want to. Very much."

"Excuse us, please, Nathan," broke in the fiercely

mustachioed gentleman across the table, speaking in French, "but could we take two minutes of your time to settle an argument? We need an impartial judge."

Reluctantly Nathan tore his eyes away from hers. "Of course. At your service," he answered vaguely, as if waking from a dream.

Shaken, Ashley drank some wine and tried to get a hold on herself. Although she would have admitted it to no one, she found the determination of such an attractive, masculine creature to have her, little Ashley Forrester, deeply satisfying. Yet she knew she had to resist him. To a man like Trent, she could be nothing more than an idle pastime. When he turned his attention to her again, she thought she was ready for him.

"How old are you, Ashley?" He eyed her speculatively. "Twenty-five?"

"Twenty-six."

Nathan refilled her glass and that of the woman on the other side of him. "Then you can't be as shocked as you pretend at what I've said. A woman with your looks has had other opportunities."

"When that kind of opportunity knocks, I don't answer," she responded. "Certainly not," she added under her breath, "after Clay."

The muscles in his jaw tensed. "Clay? You said Clay?"

Suddenly there was a wall of ice between them.

"Yes," she confessed. "I'm the 'precocious cub reporter' he nearly married."

Nathan laughed shortly. "So you're the one. And I thought my days of sharing women with Clayton were over."

"What makes you think they aren't? I'm through with him and I never started with you!" Ashley declared so loudly that several heads turned.

Ignoring her outburst, for a time he looked away toward the garden, thinking. Then he shook his head in disgust. "Yes," he said half to himself, "this has all the hallmarks of a Pridemore practical joke, and I was nearly taken in. The question is, was the lady?"

"Was the lady what?"

"Were you taken in too? Are you Clay's accomplice or merely his dupe?"

"I have no idea what you're talking about."

Nathan waited until the next course had been served before continuing. When he looked at her again, the enormous magnetism that had been building between them had dissipated. Like two stone statues they faced each other.

"Let me explain," he said coldly. "Clayton sent you here to accomplish one of two aims, if not both. Either you would write a story about me, which would annoy me because I hate publicity. Or we would—what is the discreet way to put it?—become romantically involved. Then Clay would crook his little finger, you would go running back to him, and he could have a good laugh on his old nemesis. He would win either way."

"That is the most preposterous thing I've ever heard!" Ashley exclaimed. "Clay didn't send me. It was my idea."

"How did you know to come to the restaurant?"

"He told me you always came there for lunch on Saturdays. But—"

"You see?" Nathan nodded. "And whose idea was it for you to write a series of travel articles, starting in Marseilles? It's highly irregular for a paper the size of the *Chronicle* to have its own travel writer when it could rely on wire stories."

"Oh, that was the editor of the lifestyle section," Ashley said with relief. But her relief was short-lived. "No," she admitted, "I remember now. The original idea came down from Clay's office."

"Just as I thought," Nathan said triumphantly.

"Now wait a minute," Ashley fought back. "You've assumed Clay has some hold on me, that I still feel something for him. And that's just not true."

"How long ago did you break off with him?"

"Six months ago."

"And have you dated since then?" Nathan demanded.

Ashley shook her head. "No," she said finally, "I haven't. I haven't wanted to."

"And you're trying to tell me you don't still have feelings for him?" Nathan asked almost gently. "Think about it, Ashley. Think very carefully about what I've said. I know Clayton well and I know what he's capable of."

Stunned, Ashley cut a delicate pink slice of lamb into tiny pieces and pushed them around her plate. As Nathan drifted into conversation with the others, she tried to sort out the evidence. What Nathan had said had first seemed crazy, but now she saw that there was a kind of mad logic to the alleged scheme—Clay's kind of logic. She recalled her last conversation with him, in which he had urged her to take the European assignment. The subject of Nathan had come up, as if by chance, and Clay had mentioned again the air of mystery surrounding the man and—yes, he had remarked on how little had been written about him and what a coup it would be to get a story. He had made Nathan sound like just the kind of challenge that appealed to her. She sat back. Could it be true? Had the idea not been hers at all? Had she been totally manipulated by Clay? Other remarks came back to her, insinuations she needed time to think about now. And Nathan himself seemed so sure . . .

"Excuse me," she said in confusion. "I think I should leave. Under the circumstances, I don't think it's right to accept your hospitality."

He shifted around to look at her. "You admit I'm right." His eyes were hard.

"I don't admit any such thing," Ashley said with irritation. "I simply can't remain if you think I'm here under false pretenses. And . . . and I have to think about this," she finished lamely.

"Yes," Nathan said, "you're feeling the sting of what I've said. It's true, isn't it, my beautiful enemy agent? Well," he concluded as he got to his feet, "at least you have the decency to bow out. I'll call a taxi." He excused himself and was gone.

By the time the taxi arrived, the guests were moving inside for coffee. Ashley found Charles as soon as she could.

"I'm leaving now, Charlie. You stay on and have a good time."

"What's this?" Charles, lounging on a divan, stirred the coffee in his Sèvres demitasse. "It's still early yet."

"I know, but I have packing to do and I feel a little dizzy. Must have eaten the wrong thing for lunch." She put on a brave smile. "Now, don't argue with me. I'm perfectly capable of getting back to the hotel by myself."

"You're really serious, aren't you?" Charles said with more interest. "Is anything wrong? I saw you deep in conversation with the boss."

"Everything's fine. I just want to go." She saw Nathan approaching, his arm around Renata. They looked contented and easy with one another. Damn the man!

"Then I'll see you tomorrow morning. I still insist on

taking you to the train," Charles reminded her.

"Your taxi is here." Nathan held out his hand, his gaze somewhere above her head. "Happy writing and a safe journey home, Miss Forrester. And say hello to Clayton Pridemore when you get back to the *Chronicle*."

"It was very kind of you to invite me. The dinner was lovely," she managed to say.

His handshake was wooden. Suddenly she felt a stab of regret. She would never see him again. She would never know what might have happened if Clay's name hadn't come up. She would never feel again the thrill of those formal yet disturbingly intimate kisses. *Look at me,* she screamed inside. *Let me see what you're feeling.* She smiled at Renata—a ghastly caricature of a smile, she knew. "It was nice meeting you."

"Yes, wasn't it?" The expensive face shone with victory. "Too bad you can't stay. Good-bye, Mademoiselle Forrester."

chapter 4

STILL DAMP FROM her bath, Ashley wrapped the light, turquoise kimono around her, tying it loosely, and sat down to brush out her hair. Early morning light, silvery as fish scales, spilled through the open window, along with the sound of a lone automobile purring down the street. She was thinking of Nathan. Several times during her fitful night's sleep she had awakened to find his face floating before her in the gloom. What had happened between Nathan and Clay to create such mutual suspicion and dislike? Was it true that Clay had been trying to use her to hurt Nathan? She still had no firm answers. Ashley's brow darkened. It would not be easy to wound such a hard-shelled egotist as Nathan, a man who had confidently propositioned her on the strength of a few minutes of conversation. Perhaps he and Clay were simply too much alike to be comfortable with each other. Ashley tossed the hairbrush into her open suitcase. She needn't waste any sympathy on either of them. In the cold light of morning, her only regret was that she would not have the chance to convince Nathan of her own innocence in the affair. She disliked the idea of being linked in his mind—or anyone's—with any deception.

A car door slammed in the street and she checked the travel clock on the night table. Too early for Charles. She stood and stretched luxuriantly, feeling a thrill of excitement at what lay ahead—Cannes, Antibes, Nice, Monaco—places she had long dreamed of seeing. A few hours on the fabled beaches would banish Nathan Trent from her thoughts. Perhaps she might even meet a man who was both charming and humble.

A knock at the door. It had to be the concierge, who had been told to bring her breakfast early. Holding the kimono closed at the neck, Ashley shot back the bolt and opened the door just wide enough to take the tray.

Nathan pushed his way past her. His hair was wind-blown and he appeared to have dressed hastily in rope-soled shoes, jeans, and a white silk shirt open at the neck.

"I couldn't get you out of my mind. I had to see you again." He took her by the shoulders and held her out from him. "The hell with Pridemore. I was a fool to let the past play any part in this." His eyes ran down her, appreciating the way the shiny fabric molded itself to her moist body and lingering on a bead of water trembling in the cleft of her breasts. "You look like the morning sun," he said at last, "with your hair spread out on your shoulders like that."

"Why the sudden change? What do you want?" Her heart flailed at her ribs like a frantic sparrow.

"You." His mouth came down over hers, and the heat of his hands, moving slowly and soothingly on her back, made her feel as if she were wearing nothing at all. Weakly she pushed at him, trying to break away, trying to resist both his strength and her own sudden hunger for the taste of him, which took her by surprise. "Forget the train," he murmured against her mouth. "Stay with me. I'm only asking for a day." His hands slid down, over the curve of her buttocks.

With a superhuman effort, she wrenched herself away from him. "Only a day? Only twenty-four hours? Not twenty-five or twenty-six?"

"I didn't say that."

"Yes, you did." She whirled to face him again. "One night and good-bye."

"Maybe after one night you won't want to leave at all." He took a step toward her, holding out a hand.

"Oh, no." Her robe was coming open and she adjusted the sash angrily. "You're moving too fast, way too fast. You see, Nathan, you don't know me. I have this big character flaw—I can't do anything by halves. I can't give half of myself—or one night of me. I know it's unfashionable these days, but there it is. I give all or nothing. And in this case—on such short notice," she put in sarcastically "—it has to be nothing."

"Are you sure? I'll take whatever you want to hand out," he said with a roguish grin.

"I'm not joking!" She flung back her hair and glared at him in defiance.

"Neither am I, as I said last night." He caught her gently by the wrists. "I'm not just talking about making love to you. I want to get to know you."

"Oh, please!" Ashley laughed. "I'm not going to fall for that one."

"It's true. You intrigue me. And I don't care about your original motives for coming here. I'll change them." He separated her wrists and brought them around behind his back so that she was embracing him, her body flat against his. "But don't tell me you don't like this. I can feel you liking it."

"I hope you didn't wake Renata when you rolled out of bed so early," Ashley spat at him, still fighting down desire.

"No..." his mouth plucked a slow kiss from hers "...for the very good reason..." he bent to plant a kiss in the hollow of her throat "...that she wasn't..." his lips moved down between her breasts and Ashley shivered as his tongue licked away the droplet of water ". . . in my bed."

"I don't believe you!" She twisted this way and that, fighting to get free, even as another part of her ached to give in.

"Come and see. Come home with me," he coaxed, nuzzling her.

"It doesn't matter anymore that I was Clay's fiancée?"

The effect was instantaneous. He stepped back, his chest heaving. "I'll forget about it if you will." But he sounded less sure of himself.

"What is it between you two?" Unable to keep still and wanting to put some distance between them, Ashley began wandering around the room, checking drawers and throwing the last few items into her suitcases.

Nathan flung himself into an armchair. "All right, let's get Clay settled once and for all. It's an old rivalry. Nothing that should matter now." He ran a hand through his hair. "When I decided to follow my father into the newspaper business, it seemed sensible to learn more about it than could be learned in the executive suite. I first met Clay when I was doing a stint chasing ambulances and fire engines in Cleveland. He was just starting out too, and we used to compete for stories. Later we roomed together and the competitiveness spread to other parts of our lives."

"Such as women."

"Women, tennis, whatever. For a long time we kept it friendly. I won some and he won some. But Clay could never forget that I was a Trent. It started to eat at him, and before long he saw favoritism in every one of my successes. Nothing could convince him that I was on my own." Nathan stood and paced the faded carpet. "My father and grandfather were hard-nosed about training me. While I was a reporter they wouldn't give me so much as a quarter for a phone call, and I'm grateful to them for it. I learned everything the hard way. But Clay always thought I had an unfair advantage, even though sometimes I used another name so nobody would know who I was. Finally I broke a big story about corruption in the shipping industry on the Great Lakes. The series won an award, and Clay, out of jealousy, charged that I had used my family's position, first to get the necessary information and then to win the award. When he was proven wrong—in public—it shattered our friendship. After that we left each other alone. Until now, it seems."

Ignoring the innuendo, Ashley sat down on the edge of the bed. "But you put him in charge at the *Chronicle*. Why? Out of guilt?"

Nathan shrugged. "Maybe to a degree. Perhaps because Clay was right that I'd never have to dig ditches for a living. But Clay's also a crack editor. I tried to separate the personal considerations from the professional and offer him a position worthy of his skills. He knew it was no favor when he accepted." He took the chair facing her. "But now you can understand that when you said you'd been involved with Clay, it all came back again. It was too coincidental."

"Nathan, I swear he didn't send me. I've been up half the night thinking about what you said," Ashley said seriously. "I have to admit that your theory sounds plausible. But if he were using me, I didn't know it."

"After you left last night, I came to that tentative conclusion," said Nathan. "Now, looking at you, I know I was right. You have a kind of innocence about you that's not often found in Clay's friends. Not often found in anyone."

Touched, Ashley said nothing.

"Ashley, look at me. Are you over him?"

Instead, she looked at the clock. "I need to dress. It's not long before my train."

"Your train leaves at seven fifty-seven. There's plenty of time. I asked you a question." Nathan sat forward, so that their knees touched. It was impossible to avoid his probing eyes.

Ashley swallowed. "Yes, I am over him. But I was badly hurt. Before Clay, I dated a lot and had some semiserious relationships. But nothing like a full commitment. Clay was the first . . . the first for everything." She looked down at the floor. Yet it was easier to talk about than she would have expected. Taking a deep breath, she went on. "If I hadn't been so inexperienced with men, I suppose I would have realized earlier that I wasn't the only one in his life. Or maybe I did see the warning signals and I ignored them. At any rate, one day when I went over to his apartment to take some wedding gifts, I found a strange earring in the bathroom, and I couldn't ignore the signs anymore. I couldn't accept that. My nature is to be faithful and I would expect my husband to be. Sometimes I wonder why Clay wanted marriage at all."

"Because he knows a good thing when he sees it, and so do I. Which brings us back to the problem at hand."

"Don't you understand what I'm telling you?" Ashley beseeched him. "I wasted three years of my life on a disastrous relationship. During that period I didn't give a thought to my career. I just marked time. Now I'm ready to go forward, and this trip is very important to me. It's a kind of test I've set for myself—to do something first-rate, to do it on time, and to use it to get a better job elsewhere. I've been writing well and I don't want to break that momentum. As a professional, you can understand that." She went to the window and for a few moments let the breeze bathe her hot face. With her back to him, it was easier to say, "I can't afford to take any more detours, not even for one night. Or rather, especially not for one night."

"One always finds time to do the things one really wants to do."

Ashley watched an old woman come out of the bakery across the street with four long, crusty loaves caught loosely under one arm like sticks of kindling. Could she trust Nathan not to hurt her? After Clay, could she trust any man? Suddenly a chilling thought occurred to her.

"You've questioned my motives," she said with a sinking heart. "Perhaps I should question yours. Maybe I'm just a pawn in another competition between you and Clay. Is that why you came? To show Clay how easily you can conquer 'his' girl? Am I first prize in the latest contest between you?"

"Leave Clay out of this!" Nathan roared behind her. "There is no contest. This is between you and me!"

"There's nothing between you and me, Nathan." Ashley was convinced that her hunch was right. "I've had enough pain. I don't want any more."

Nathan spun her around, lightning and thunder in his face. But his voice was cool and measured. "You think you've suffered, don't you? Your lover was unfaithful, so you're wearing your poor little broken heart on your sleeve so the whole world will feel sorry for you."

"I happen to take those things seriously."

Nathan looked down at her with a strange expression that was half pity and half annoyance. "You think that's serious, do you? Was anybody killed or maimed? Did you lose anything irreplaceable?"

"No, but it was tragic enough, thank you." Stepping

around him, she gathered up her clothes. "Excuse me, but Charles is going to be here any minute to take me to the train. Your little game will have to be cancelled."

As she bent over a suitcase, she heard him cross the room. Then, in a new, hollow voice, he said, "Don't tell me about pain. And don't tell me about keeping to schedules. Because you haven't really felt the pain of love and you don't really know how precious time is."

The door slammed behind him.

Ashley stood frozen as the sincere emotion behind his last words sank in. Had she been wrong about him?

"Wait!" She flew to the door and threw it open. "Wait!" She ran to the head of the stairs and looked down the stairwell to the ground floor, hearing his fast, staccato steps but unable to see him. "Nathan, please!"

No answer.

Down the hall, someone stuck his head out and shouted at her. Ashley ran back to her window and leaned out. Nathan was getting into a silver sports car.

"Nathan! What did you mean? I don't understand."

He glanced up with no emotion. "No," he said just loud enough for her to hear, "you don't."

The car shot down the street like a bullet.

A short while later, when Ashley and Charles were en route to the train station, she said, "Tell me something. Was Nathan Trent ever in a serious accident?"

"You noticed his face and the limp," Charles guessed.

"Yes, that's it," Ashley returned, deciding to keep Nathan's visit to herself. "What happened?"

"I was going to mention it the other day in the office," Charles said. "Not many people remember it these days, but there was a lot of publicity at the time. In fact, that may be where Trent got his dislike of reporters. It must have happened seven or eight years ago. Nathan was on his honeymoon in Switzerland."

"He was *married?*"

"Not for long." Charles maneuvered the little Simca around a truck. "Her name was Ingrid, I think, and she was Danish. A lovely girl, by all accounts. She and Nathan were married quietly here in Marseilles and went to the Swiss Alps for a long honeymoon. They both liked mountain climbing. One afternoon they were out on a difficult but supposedly safe trail with a guide and were caught in an avalanche. I don't remember the details, except that they were caught in a pass and there was no way to escape. Nathan's wife and the guide were killed. He miraculously survived but spent weeks in the hospital with two broken legs and internal injuries. He never talks about it. Never."

"I know," Ashley said softly.

"What?"

"Oh, nothing." Nathan was right, she thought. She didn't understand. And he couldn't tell her. He couldn't cheapen a thing like that by using it to win a point in an argument. And now they had both lost something.

"There's the station," said Charles cheerfully. "I'll bet you can hardly wait to get on your way."

As the train moved slowly out of the station, Ashley waved blankly to Charles from the window of her coach, not seeing him, not seeing anyone but Nathan, who was not there.

chapter 5

"Buon giorno. I am Signora De Lucca." Resting her tray on the edge of the small window table, the woman set out a porcelain pitcher of black coffee, a larger one containing frothing hot milk, and a basket of crusty rolls. Then she rummaged in an apron pocket and brought forth an airmail envelope. "Here it is. My husband forgot to give it to you last night when you arrived." Before handing it over, she surveyed the table with a critical eye. "Is there anything else you would like? There are soft-boiled eggs... for a slight surcharge, of course...."

Glowing from a good night's sleep and a week of Riviera sun, Ashley shook her head as she accepted the envelope. "No, thank you," she said, "this is fine. Besides, I want to get started sightseeing as soon as possible." She patted the guidebook and camera beside her plate.

Signora De Lucca was a large, cushiony woman with shrewd but kindly eyes. Now she fixed them on Ashley in speculation. "But where are you going at this hour? Nothing is open. It's much too early." To prove her point, she indicated with a sweep of her arm the otherwise deserted dining room of the Pensione De Lucca. "Excuse me for asking questions," she added with an ingratiating smile, "but my guests are like my family."

Ashley poured coffee. "I want to get the feeling of Rome without the tourists. I thought I'd walk over to the Colosseum."

"The Colosseum?" The woman pursed her lips and

considered Ashley's answer before saying hesitantly, "Perhaps you don't understand, Miss. These old ruins, they're not the kind of place for a young woman alone. Especially not for one like you—one so *bella*, so beautiful. In recent years, at the wrong time of day, they have been—" She stopped, searching for words, then brightened. "There are three American students in room 204. Nice girls. You can wait and go along with them, no? Would you like for me to arrange it?"

"Thank you, but I can take care of myself," Ashley said pleasantly but firmly. "The point is I'm a journalist and I like seeing things from an uncommon perspective. I want to go alone. It's my choice."

"All right," Signora De Lucca said, not unkindly. "It's not my business." She shrugged and picked up her tray. "But I hope there is a special saint who watches over Americans."

Busybody, Ashley grumbled to herself. It's a public place. Anyway, I'm not beautiful. Just ask Clay. She opened the letter. It was from Trudy, her editor at the *Chronicle*.

> Congrats on the stories from Marseilles. Both the one on the Vieux Port and the other about the street markets are just what we wanted—crisp and colorful. Also received the third—about the perfume industry around Grasse—and we'll run it tomorrow. Clay seemed to think you would stay longer in Marseilles, though. He's been seen in the company of the new girl in advertising, by the way, but I guess all the office gossip will keep until you get back. Hope this reaches you before you start for home. Meanwhile, when in Rome, do as the Romans do. That should give you enough to write about!

Ashley shoved the letter into the pocket of her slacks. Too bad your little plan didn't work, Clay dear, she thought bitterly. Too bad Nathan isn't as big a fool as I am. She drummed her fingers on the edge of the table in annoyance. She had promised herself she would not think about Nathan, and she had been nearly as good as her word for a whole week. The one time he did come to mind, when a tall man with blue eyes had passed her on the beach at Nice, she had convinced herself that Nathan's face and voice were already growing hazy. But now, suddenly, details came flooding back—the crooked, sardonic smile; the small white scar that hid in one eyebrow; the smooth, careless way he moved. And above all, above everything, the way they felt together when he held her. They had been so near to something and yet so far away. . . .

Two other guests arrived and Ashley forced herself back to the present. The man and woman took the other window table next to hers, nodding a polite greeting. With their soft white hair, pink cheeks, and gentle countenances, they looked like a pair of elderly angels in sensible shoes, come to pay reverence to the Eternal City. But their presence also reminded Ashley of the hordes of tourists that must even now be loading their cameras and boarding their buses. She finished quickly. All of Rome was waiting. She had no time for regrets.

Outside, the sky was an explosion of color. Soaring streaks of pink, gold, and blue washed the clear ocean upon which sailed towering white clouds. Ashley's spirits rose with the rising sun. Rome, time scarred yet forever young, saint and courtesan, fallen ruler of the Western world. For an hour Ashley Forrester would be its only tourist. Map in hand, she swung along the empty streets, her senses alive to everything—to the smell of warm bread from an open doorway, to the splash of color on a flowered balcony, to the muffled roar—like the surge of the sea—that was the sound of a great city breathing. The driver of a passing truck waved and honked. She laughed and waved back.

"Rome," she said aloud, beginning to compose her next story, "is a stirring chorus in stone. Ancient stones that chant in faded ocher, russet, and umber; and new stones shouting in alabaster and pewter." A stray cat on a wall caught her in a merciless glare, and she said to it, "The same cobblestones that a tourist walks on today were once trod by Caesars and Borgias and popes. And the message they sound out is this: Life goes on. Whatever happens, life goes on." Ahead she saw her destination brooding against the fresh sky. Clayton Pridemore, Nathan Trent, she added silently. What were they to her? Acquaintances of a moment, mere sparks of time. And now, life went on. She increased her pace, feeling joyous and free. This was the independence she had come to Europe to regain. It was the way she used to be, before Clay.

Not ten minutes later, as she stood beneath the craggy, pitted walls of one of Europe's most famous landmarks, words failed her. Awed by its decayed majesty, remembering having read about the horrible contests it had witnessed—wild beasts tearing each other to pieces and gladiators hacking and bludgeoning each other for the entertainment of the masses—she stood unmoving for a time. Then, with an effort, she took out her notebook and began to stroll around the circumference, taking down ideas and descriptions. She had been right about one thing—it was a place to savor alone. But Signora De Lucca had been right also. It appeared that Ashley had arrived too early to see the interior.

But just as she was putting away her pen and thinking of visiting the nearby Arch of Constantine, a workman carrying a ladder came sauntering around the bend of the walls.

Ashley hurried to meet him. *"Entrata?"* she asked, pointing to an arched entranceway. "May I go in?"

The workman regarded her without interest. Mumbling a refusal, he hitched the ladder higher on his shoulder and started to move on.

Ashley produced a roll of thousand-lire notes and peeled off two. *"Per favore.* Please."

The man adjusted his greasy cap, scratched his cheek, and looked to the right and left. He held out his hand. In one minute Ashley was inside. In two, she had found her way to a position midway up the side of the amphitheater and was looking down on the fabled arena, congratulating herself on her resourcefulness.

Much of the floor of the arena had been excavated to show the underground rooms where the animals and combatants had been kept until their moments of trial in the ring. Ashley took out her camera and began snapping pictures of the simple cross at ground level, a memorial to the Christian martyrs. She also shot the first rows of seats, where the emperor had sat and before which the gladiators halted in their entrance procession to deliver the famous greeting, *Morituri te salutamus:* we who are about to die salute you. Then, as she panned the camera across the opposite side of the Colosseum, she saw something move in one of the exits.

A man was watching her from the shadows. There was something furtive in his manner that she did not like. As she lowered the camera, he stepped further into the light, ogling her boldly. She stilled a flutter of alarm and went back to note taking. There was plenty of distance between them. Besides, his presence must mean that others were arriving. The next time she glanced up, he had disappeared and she put him out of her mind.

Seconds later, however, he appeared in another doorway, this time considerably closer to her. He was a pudgy specimen of middle age with a day's growth of beard and black hair that lay flat as paint on his round head. She saw his lips move and knew that he was speaking to her. Then he vanished again.

Outside the Colosseum, the traffic of modern Rome was building toward morning rush hour, but inside, an ancient, eerie stillness reigned. Ashley strained to hear footsteps. When she heard none, her mouth went dry. Where had he gone? Where was the workman? Where was anybody? She looked around nervously. She appeared to be alone. Maybe she had imagined his interest. She tried to concentrate on the structure of the stadium. The opening at the end of the arena must be the Death Gate. . . .

The man now stood not twenty feet away, devouring her with his eyes. His face had gone sickly slack, and there was something indefinably obscene about his stance.

Still more annoyed than alarmed, Ashley stuffed camera and notebook into her shoulder bag and, as slowly and casually as she could, turned into the nearest exit. The sudden change from sunlight to dark cost her an instant's panic before her vision adjusted itself, and she stumbled noisily on the stairs. But she went on and soon reached ground level. Hearing voices somewhere to the left, she allowed herself a small sigh of relief, then began to walk toward them. The crisis had been avoided.

She was in a dim gallery or passageway that circled the interior of the Colosseum. A series of columns connected by arches curved into the obscurity in front of her and she walked along them rapidly. The voices had ceased. Risking a glance over her shoulder, she saw only purplish shadows hanging in wavering veils from the ceiling. The fat man must be waiting upstairs for a more willing victim. Or perhaps, she admitted, he had only been trying to start a conversation after all. Perhaps she had overreacted to the smell of senseless cruelty that still lingered about the place even after so many centuries.

She gasped as the man stepped from behind a column in front of her. He said something brief and brutal. Then he side-stepped twice, to place himself squarely in her path.

"Go away! Leave me alone!" Ashley shouted. And it was that, the unexpected, naked terror in her own voice, that made her truly frightened for the first time. "Get away from me!" she screamed.

He started toward her, in the flat-footed gait of the congenitally obese, an oily sheen of determination lighting his crude features. The fingers of one hand flexed mechanically. Half running and half walking, Ashley turned and fled. She had lost all sense of direction in the circular structure. Was she going toward the exit or away from it? What had happened to the voices? She cursed herself for not listening to Signora De Lucca and broke into a full-fledged run as, behind her, the heavy footfalls quickened.

Her throat began to ache and her breath came in long gasps that sounded like silk tearing. It had just occurred to her that she might have overshot the exit, that they might circle forever, like the condemned in a Dantesque hell, when she saw, several yards ahead, a shaft of light falling across the stones. A way out! Outside he wouldn't dare! She plunged into the hot sunlight and slowed to a walk, her chest heaving.

She found herself in a wide, bare parking area that isolated the Colosseum in the middle of the Piazza di Colosseo. Around that island streaked a thick band of rush-hour traffic, so swift and deafening that the Colosseum resembled a gigantic hive beset by a swarm of killer bees. Discovering no way to reach the buildings on the other side, she realized with a shock that her danger was just as great as before.

Ashley's pursuer hung back, jackallike, as if to allow her time to appreciate the extent of her helplessness. When he spoke again, this time low and crooning, she turned on him in a fury.

"I told you to leave me alone!" She made a shooing motion. "Go on now!"

To her astonishment, with a wet grin he turned and went. Ashley raised a trembling hand and wiped the sweat out of her eyes. She watched him until he had shuffled out of sight around the curve of the Colosseum. Then she began to walk slowly and unsteadily in the opposite direction, on the lookout for a way across the murderous traffic. Never again, she thought dully. Never, never again. She stopped to take some slow, deep breaths. That was when she heard the motor start.

A small, dirty tin can of a car came tearing into view, the fat man at the wheel. Once he had her in his sights, he barreled straight toward her, accelerating. She had to move, yet there was nowhere to go. Tears of frustration blinding her, she stumbled in a zigzag course toward the traffic. A scene from a travelogue flashed through her mind—that of a lone gazelle being chased across the African veldt by a Land Rover full of hunters. Out of

the corner of her eye she saw the automobile closing in
on her. She felt the heat of the engine, like the panting
of a beast of prey, hot on her hip. The next thing she
knew, a hand pawed at her and took hold of her shirt
pocket. Her persecutor leaned halfway out the window,
driving recklessly with the other hand, his face so close
that she could see the details of his bad teeth. With all
the force that fear lent, she threw herself backward and
heard the thin cotton rip as the pocket flew off. She fell
heavily to the ground, landing on her elbows and the
base of her spine.

The car stopped on a dime. With an agility surprising
in a man so shapeless, the driver leapt out and rushed
for her. Ashley staggered to her feet and ran toward the
streaming traffic. Brought up short at its edge, for an
instant she waved her arms wildly, trying to attract attention. But the commuters no more noticed her than the
drivers in a chariot race notice the birds in the trees.
She looked back at the awful smile looming nearer and
nearer, then flung herself from the curb, into the path
of a Volkswagen truck.

Brakes squealed and horns blared. Cars swerved and
skidded. People shouted and shook their fists. Ashley
ran heedlessly, crossing lane after lane, jumping back
once when a fender grazed her thigh. Exhaust fumes
choked her; tears stung her. At the sound of shattering
glass, she turned and saw the dirty little car stranded
broadside in the swirling melee. Then she was running
up a wooded slope, and someone, a ticket taker or care-
taker perhaps, ran out of a building and called after her.
She didn't care. Pushed on by the cacophony on the
highway, which was like a gale at her back, she continued
to race upward, now on grass. At last, when the stitch

in her side would allow her to go no farther, she fell against a tree, circling it with her arms for support, and looked down.

She was high enough to see the entire piazza spread out below her. Ironically, the first tour bus of the day was disgorging its passengers in front of the Colosseum. Her nemesis was nowhere in sight. No doubt, she prayed, he had joined the flow of traffic, which was steady again and looked as if it had never been interrupted. And indeed, she fancied that she saw the little car vanishing down a boulevard. A sob of relief constricted her throat.

With clumsy fingers Ashley raked back her hair, which hung in tangled ringlets about her face. Her whole body was as taut as a high-tension wire, and she felt a cold tingling in her nostrils that signaled that she was about to faint. A broken Doric column lay across the hillside a few feet away, and she collapsed gratefully upon it, lowering her head between her knees until she felt in control of herself again. Then she took inventory. Her face in the mirror of her compact was dust streaked and ghastly pale. She scrubbed away the worst with her handkerchief. Her slacks were smudged from her fall, and a dark gray streak told of her brief encounter with the fender of the Fiat. Miraculously, she still had her shoulder bag. The right patch pocket of her peach-colored shirt had been torn off neatly, without causing further damage to the shirt. But she saw that she would have to return to the pensione and change, for the pockets had been designed to camouflage bralessness, and now the gauzy fabric clearly revealed the shape and heft of one breast. For the moment, however, she could only sit quietly and collect herself and be thankful.

She was on the Palatine Hill, which had once been

crowded with the palaces of Republican and Imperial
Rome and where now only ruins hinted at the grandeur
that had been. Caesar Augustus had lived there, and
Caligula and Mark Antony. Every inch of ground was
sacred to the historian. According to a legend she recalled
from the research she had done before leaving University
Park, it was also the site of the den of the she-wolf that
had suckled Romulus and Remus, the founders of Rome.

A bright-green lizard spiraled up the column and
hopped into the grass. The sunlight caressed Ashley's
back like a hand. Her muscles began to relax, but not
her mind. She wondered how such a thing could have
happened to her, in the middle of a city in broad daylight.
But wasn't that just where atrocities blatantly occurred?
In cities, where criminal and victim alike were faceless,
where nobody was minding anybody else's business the
way they did in towns and villages? Yes, the more public
the place, the more deadly its small privacies. . . .

She shook herself to banish such musings. The horror
was past. She stood and found that her knees no longer
felt like buckling. For a moment she considered heading
straight back to the pensione and going to bed for the
rest of the day, but she reminded herself that the professional thing to do was to get on with her job. She could
at least see the Palatine Hill, since she was there. She
did, nevertheless, promise herself a long bath and nap
thereafter. Leafing through her guidebook, she found the
map of the Palatine ruins and picked a winding path that
led through a grove of pines, with the Farnese Gardens
as her eventual destination. As soon as she began to
walk, she felt better. What a story she could tell the
Chronicle readers!

It was as if she had entered one of the melodramatic
paintings she had seen in the museums of Marseilles, in

which a landscape dotted with classical ruins of solitary tombs, crumbling arches, and stone steps leading nowhere slowly sinks back into nature. She imagined herself as the fair, pale lady in trailing white who roams among the ruins distraught. Above there would be a thunderous, stormy sky, and a flickering along the horizon . . . and of course, in the distance, a horseman, although whether he was meant for the lady or not was unclear. . . .

Smiling at the picture her overwrought imagination was creating, Ashley slowed to study the map and to identify the weathered brick wall before her. With lowered eyes, she rounded the shattered remnant and was brought sharply to her senses by the crunch of footsteps. She stared and went cold all over. *No*, she whispered. *Oh, please, no.*

The fat man toiled up the grade toward her, his little pig eyes narrow with resolve. At the sight of her, he grunted and surged forward, his body efficiently low to the ground.

The guidebook fell from her fingers. Ashley left the path in a leap and scrambled up the hillside. Immediately she lost her footing and fell, catching herself on the heels of her hands, but she recovered and kept going. Madly trying to remember the map she had pored over moments before, she dodged an excavation site that gaped suddenly at her feet and skirted a low, broken wall. There were stairs somewhere that led down to the Roman Forum. There, surely, she would find other people. And if not there, then on the adjacent Capitoline Hill, which blended into modern commercial Rome. If, that is, she lasted that long. As she ran, she berated herself for being so stupid as to have relaxed her guard. Never again? How soon she had forgotten!

Ahead she saw a sprawling, roofless jumble of walls. A palace, she thought, where perhaps she could lose him in a maze of rooms. Then, with nauseating force, it dawned on her that she was more likely to lose herself, and in more ways than one. Her pursuer seemed to know the terrain perfectly, as if he hunted there often. One backward glimpse told her he was bounding along as nimbly as a mountain goat and that he was gaining. Nevertheless, when she came to the rubbled terrace she did not hesitate but dashed across it and through an open doorway. Darting aimlessly, in and out of openings and up and down steps, she fled from one bare suggestion of a room to another, until suddenly she realized that she was no longer being followed. She stopped to listen. Somewhere leaves rustled in a breeze. A bird trilled. Nothing more. She let out her breath slowly. Blind white eyes on a fragmented frieze gazed coldly down on her.

Then she heard not one but two sets of footsteps approaching. Her heart froze. Did he have an accomplice? Both sets of steps intermittently progressed and hesitated, as if their owners, too, were listening. They were coming from opposite directions.

To her despair, Ashley found that she had entered a cul-de-sac. At her back was a long drop to a sunken terrace or garden, a drop she could never survive. On either side of her were walls. In front of her was another wall with a jagged breach, through which she had come. She considered shouting for help, but was help out there, or double danger? It was too big a risk to take. She knelt, scooped up a handful of stones and, squaring her shoulders, stepped through the narrow passageway. From the left something lunged at her. She let fly with the stones, and the fat man recoiled with a growl as they spattered his face. Instinctively she wheeled. When she collided with the other dim, hulking figure, she broke into wild sobs and beat at the arms that encircled her like iron bands, crushing her against a hard chest.

"Well, well," she heard Nathan's voice say, "if it isn't little Miss American Independence."

chapter 6

"NATHAN, NATHAN," ASHLEY sobbed over and over, her face buried in his shirt and her arms solidly around him. It was like holding on to a tree, the sturdiest oak in the world. Above her head a volley of Italian flew at the fat man, and she felt, rather than saw, him cringe and slink away like the cur that he was. Then Nathan began to stroke her hair, slowly and tenderly. After a time Ashley looked up at him. When their eyes met, it was like coming home.

"This isn't a coincidence, is it?" she managed to ask at last.

"No, damn it, it isn't." His face held a mixture of annoyance, relief, and something else that she might, in another man, have called affection. But Nathan neither had any reason to feel affection for her nor was he the affectionate type. "What the devil do you mean by roaming around on your own like this?" he demanded.

"I . . . I wanted to see a different Rome than others see. To have a unique experience."

"Darling," he chuckled, brushing a lock of hair back from her eyes, "if you want to have a unique experience in Rome, I can give it to you."

"Can I take a rain check? I think I've had enough uniqueness for one day," she tried to banter back as she let go of him. At once her head became as light and empty as the shell of a gourd. "I lost my guidebook," she said vaguely. "I'll have to find it . . ." She took a step that seemed to land on thin air, and the next step never landed at all, for as she fell, Nathan caught her behind her knees and lifted her as easily as if she were a child.

"You're hyperventilating," he said against her cheek. "Hold your breath for ten seconds."

"I'm fine," she protested feebly as she struggled to raise her head. "You don't have to——" But it was such a relief to be surrounded by his strength and warmth that she did not finish. She only opened her eyes when Nathan set her down on a stone bench some distance from the ruins.

Taking a seat beside her, he watched her with grave attention. Gradually Ashley felt the color come back to her face and steadiness return to her limbs. She sat up straight, feeling foolish.

Nathan touched her cheek and hands. "You're cold." He frowned. "Are you all right? Are you injured anywhere? Do you need a doctor?"

Ashley regarded the furrows of concern across his brow with surprise. Her head was as clear as a bell again, but she could not fathom the reason for Nathan's presence, much less his solicitude. Could his ego simply not tolerate the kind of parting they'd had in Marseilles? It didn't make any sense.

"Of course I'm all right," she said brusquely, for she suddenly remembered that this was the second time he was seeing her at a disadvantage where her reporting was concerned, the first being her inept attempt to interview him in the restaurant in Marseilles. "You don't have to look so worried. I was just frightened, that's all. All I need is to change this shirt and find my guidebook, and I can pick up where I left off. I hardly got started with my notes. Are you on your way somewhere?"

"Oh, sure." His voice was curt as he turned away. Resting his elbows on his knees, he looked down at the ground and appeared to be arguing with himself.

A file of marble columns marched across the hillside in front of them. The masses of purple spikes at their bases must be, Ashley decided, the legendary acanthus flower. She looked out over Rome, which stretched before them like an intricate carpet pattern, and saw the dome of St. Peter's rising out of the haze. Independence was fine, she reflected, but how much richer the view when there was someone to share it with. Or were they sharing anything? She cast a covert glance at Nathan's brooding profile. He was wearing a beige linen suit, a white shirt, a tie in an exquisitely subtle weave, and expensive loafers, all in all giving the impression of being dressed for an important meeting. How in the world had he turned up in the ruins of the Domus Augustana, or wherever they were, and exactly why?

"The word *palace* actually came from this hill we're on, the Palatine," he said abruptly in the manner of a tour guide, "and that breeze you're feeling is one of the main reasons the Romans built their palaces up here. It was marshy and humid below, you see." He shot her a look of disgust. "Or do you already have all of this in your notes?"

Stung, Ashley touched his arm. "I guess I haven't really thanked you. I don't want to think about what might have happened if you hadn't come along." She shuddered. "For the first time I really understand the phrase 'a fate worse than death.'"

"Glad to be of service." He brushed back a cuff and checked his watch. "I suppose I've taken up enough of your time," he said with biting sarcasm, and stood up to go.

Ashley leapt to her feet. "How can you say such a thing? You can't just leave! I don't even know why you're here!"

"The *Mediterranean Report* has a Rome bureau," he said, "so let's just say I came to Rome on business. I often do. Now you tend to your business and I'll tend to mine."

"But *here*. Where I am."

He ran a hand through his hair. "Okay," he said, facing her again, "I'll tell you. After I left your hotel in Marseilles, I sent for the file of stories you'd written for the *Chronicle*. I read all of them, every last one—the story on the old woman in the nursing home, the one about the little boy with leukemia, the pet show, the family of circus performers—every word. Yesterday afternoon, when I finished, I knew I wanted to know more about the woman who had written them. Because that woman has a heart and soul. So, I came looking for her." His nostrils flared. "Now I'm not sure I'll ever find her."

"What do you mean?" The anger he was barely holding in check baffled her.

"Maybe that's what happens to your heart and soul. Maybe it all goes into your work. The Ashley Forrester I've found—the same one I met in Marseilles, incidentally—doesn't have much left over for people."

"That's not true!" she countered. "You know I'm very grateful to you—"

"Exactly," he snorted. "You're grateful because I ran your friend off. The fact that I've come here, chasing after you like a kid, doesn't matter. Now I can get the hell out and let you get on with your itinerary."

"Don't you dare throw my career up to me again!" Ashley snapped. "A man who's really strong isn't threatened by that."

"Your career isn't the issue," he sneered. "You only use that as an excuse for having everything your own way. I've seen your type before, honey. You want a man who'll be weak as long as you feel like being strong and who'll be. strong when you feel like being weak. You were willing enough to lean on me a few minutes ago, but now that you've got your nerve back, it's over. That's not liberation, it's manipulation. Sorry, but I'm just not that accommodating." He started to go, then turned around. "Maybe you should give Clay another whirl. Maybe he'd fit on your leash better than I do."

Her palm cracked against his cheek like a shot.

Before she could draw back her hand, Nathan caught her wrist and twisted her arm behind her. His face contorted in rage, he bent her slowly back over the stone bench until her body was arched against his.

Wordlessly Ashley stared into the deep, drowning blue of his eyes, wanting with all her strength to slap him again. But at the feel of him down the length of her torso, a flame began to curl inside her, licking in a slow circle through her pelvis. Of its own accord her body arched more sharply against him, and she saw the emotion in his face change, flowing over the fine line between fury and desire. As his eyes dropped to her right breast, where the aureole showed rosily through the single layer of cloth, her nipples grew taut, straining against the fabric, and she thought their hot itchiness would drive her mad. His other hand went to the small of her back and he forced her upright against him. Then he kissed her neck with short, savage kisses until, unable to wait any longer to feel his mouth on hers, she freed her wrist and pulled his face to hers.

And of course, just when she least needed them, other sightseers arrived. Out of the corner of her eye, Ashley saw two figures stroll past, heads turned to watch. Pushing at Nathan's chest, she gasped, "We're becoming a spectacle."

"Maybe this is what they came to Rome to see—

amore in action," he suggested. "Do you want to say good-bye now?"

For a split second Ashley wavered, sensing that the question was much more important than his tone indicated. Was it true what he'd said about her? Did she only take, without giving? He was giving *her* something now—a second chance. Suddenly she knew she could not bear to watch him walk away. "Wherever you're going today," she said huskily, "take me with you."

"The lady's attitude is improving," Nathan said with a sly grin.

She looked at him through her lashes. "The strong woman knows when it's to her advantage to give in."

"And the strong man knows when to accept it gracefully. Shall we?" He offered his arm with a mocking flourish.

As they left, Ashley saw the elderly couple from the Pensione De Lucca watching them from another path. The two smiled benevolently and waved.

"Who are they?" asked Nathan.

"Angels," Ashley murmured. "I just *knew* they were angels."

A few minutes later, after Nathan had made a phone call, they found a taxi stand and engaged a cab. While Nathan gave directions to the driver, Ashley let her head fall back against the seat wearily. Although she had denied it to Nathan, she was suffering from the effects of her flight from the fat man. Her joints were stiffening, she had pain at the base of her spine from her fall, and her elbows and the heels of her hands smarted where she had scraped them. Yet the emotional damage was much less than she would have expected. It was, she knew, because Nathan's presence so filled her up that nothing else mattered quite as much as it had before. Even the scars Clay left had faded since Marseilles.

The taxi began to roll. Nathan still leaned forward, speaking to the driver, and Ashley let her gaze roam freely over him, noting how the continental cut of his suit emphasized the way his torso tapered from broad shoulders to trim waist and the way the hard muscles molded his thighs. She could hardly believe the strength of the physical attraction between them, having never experienced anything like it before. Even the way his hair curled over the edge of his collar made her feel weak. And he felt it too. She could sense him fighting for control, just as she was.

Ashley shifted uneasily and looked out the window. She had lived long enough to know that a man who made you feel like this didn't come along often, and maybe only once in a lifetime. She'd heard friends and older acquaintances speak of him, that man you find yourself lying awake over at three in the morning, the one whose voice you hear in every romantic song. There is one in nearly every woman's past, but he isn't the one you marry. He's too elusive, too obviously bound for another destination. Of course, once in a while one of them actually falls in love. . . .

As Nathan settled back for the ride, his thigh brushed hers and she closed her eyes, overcome by longing. What was she doing? How could the thought of marriage even enter her mind? Practically the only thing she knew for certain about Nathan's character was that he was not the marrying kind, not any more. As for herself, she was not about to build a relationship on physical attraction alone. Or to make the same mistake twice of giving up everything for a man. She would have to remind Nathan of that soon. Still, something didn't fit. He didn't have to come all the way to Rome for a willing bed partner.

He was speaking, pointing out the sights. Ashley tried

to pay attention, but a disturbing thought occurred to her, one she had had before.

"How did you find me?" she asked.

"I got your itinerary from the *Chronicle*," he answered easily. "After that, it was just a matter of finding the Pensione De Lucca. The woman there said you had gone to the Colosseum. I went there in a cab, but it wasn't open."

"I was inside," Ashley admitted. "That's where I ran into that awful man. I was lucky to get out."

"When I didn't find you," Nathan resumed, "I figured you would be either on the Palatine or in the Forum. The rest you know."

"I see." Ashley nodded slowly. So he had phoned the *Chronicle* twice. A transatlantic call from His Majesty Nathan Trent would cause a great stir. Clay would certainly be told. More than likely, he would speak to Nathan himself. Ashley studied her knees. Nathan and Clay discussing her. Placing a bet, perhaps, on Nathan's chances. Competing just like in the old days. That was what this mad dash to Rome—and his suddenly renewed interest in her—was all about.

"I've changed my mind," she said. "I want to go back to my room."

But Nathan was giving more instructions to the driver. When the cab slid over to the curb, he looked her up and down and said, "Brush the dust off your slacks. We're getting out here."

Ashley set her jaw stubbornly. "Didn't you hear what I said?"

Nathan got out of the taxi and came around to open Ashley's door. "Yes, I heard what you said. But considering that you've spent the morning trying to be the first person in modern times to be martyred in the Colosseum, I'm not letting you out of my sight." With a disarming smile he pulled her out of the car by both hands and waved the driver on.

The independent part of her was fuming, but the part of her that wanted to be pampered and taken care of had been neglected for so long that now she found Nathan's air of command nearly irresistible. In spite of all her suspicions, she ached to trust him and to lean on him. One more hour, she promised herself. One more hour. Then she would call his bluff.

"The Piazza di Spagna," Nathan announced as they came to a wide square with a fountain in the middle.

"Oh!" Ashley exclaimed. "I've always wanted to see this!" Across the piazza, the famous Spanish Steps, built of smooth travertine, flowed in a frozen cascade from the honey-colored church San Trinità dei Monti down to the festive unbrella-topped flower carts on the edge of the piazza. "And the room where Keats died. It looked out on these steps," she went on breathlessly. "And look up there, by the fountain!" She pointed to a number of fashion models in evening dress who were being photographed in a series of dramatic poses.

Nathan's eyes crinkled with amusement. He patted her arm in a proprietary way.

"Okay, okay," Ashley admitted with a shamefaced grin. "I'm glad I came along."

"And not just for the sights. I hope you like the company," he pressed.

"Y—" But she thought of his probable conversation with Clay and stopped. Instead, she nodded toward the models. "Very exotic, aren't they?"

Four tall women in metallic jersey gowns were poised around the edge of the fountain, running through a variety of stances as the cameras clicked and whirred. Their

movements were so practiced and dancelike, their poses
so difficult and unusual, that Ashley could hardly take
her eyes from them. As she and Nathan continued strolling around the piazza, however, she became aware of
a break in the fluid movement. One of the models was
standing stock still, staring in their direction. With a
shock, Ashley realized who it was. Renata. A man with
a clipboard ran up to Renata, shouting. Reluctantly the
woman began to move again, effortlessly graceful. But
even at that distance Ashley could feel the unwavering
blaze of her green eyes.

Nathan looked straight ahead. If he knew Renata was
there, he was not giving it away. But of course he knew,
Ashley seethed. Of course he could recognize his own
lover. So, she thought bitterly, he had a backup in town,
in case she didn't come through.

They turned down a street lined with expensive shops.

"Here we are," Nathan said blandly, ushering Ashley
inside a boutique with a single satin peignoir and an urn
of peacock feathers in the window.

The interior was discreetly luxurious, with striped
satin walls and a thick, dove-gray carpet. A few dresses
of simple but flawless design were displayed on stylized
mannequins scattered about the room, mingling with
potted ferns and oriental vases on plain pedestals. A slim,
gray-haired woman wearing a black dress and a gold
pince-nez glided forward to greet them.

Although Ashley could not understand the conversation, it was clear from the woman's manner that she
and Nathan had met before. When she showed them to
a sofa and went away, Ashley burst out, "Why did we
come here?"

Nathan stretched out his long legs and crossed them
at the ankles. "I thought we'd buy you a new blouse

before lunch. That one is somewhat worse for the wear."

"I don't need you to buy me blouses," Ashley said tightly. "You may remember that I asked to go back to my room, where I have other clothes. What's the matter, does my appearance embarrass you?"

A muscle jumped in his jaw, but he maintained his composure and did not look at her. "When I'm interested in a woman, I like to do nice things for her," he said quietly. "It's the most natural thing in the world. I'm interested in you, Ashley. I don't know why you can't see it. Maybe we started off the wrong way in Marseilles, but surely you realize that I wouldn't have taken the trouble to come to Rome if I hadn't changed my mind about some things. I'd like for us to start over."

She was sure he had changed his mind after he had talked to Clay. He wanted to win even more now, she thought grimly.

"It gives some men a sense of power to pursue a woman like this and spend money on her," she said carefully. "I think you should know now that I can't be bought. Money doesn't mean that much to me. I was never poor enough to crave it or rich enough to become used to it." She looked around the room. Was this where he bought Renata's clothes? Renata, who was only a few blocks away, waiting for him to whistle for her? "I'm cheap but I'm not easy," she added with a snap. "I think you like women the other way around." She stood up, but Nathan caught her wrist and pulled her back down.

"I hope you realize that you're already traveling on Trent money," he said coldly. "Where do you think the salaries at the *Chronicle* come from?"

"Yes, but I earned that!"

"Did you? How? Was this the way Clay paid you off? Did he promise you a trip to Europe if you'd set him free without causing a scandal? Maybe I'm just not offering enough."

For several seconds Ashley was too livid for words. "Damn you!" she hissed finally. "Let go of me! I'm not going to be insulted like that. And I have better things to do than fight with you all day."

"Oh, we're not going to fight all day," Nathan rejoined reasonably. He placed her hand on her knee with care. "The way I see it, we'll have one more big argument this afternoon. Then there shouldn't be another one for several days."

"Several days?"

"That's right." Nathan cocked his head at her, a half smile on his lips. "Didn't I tell you? I've upped the ante. In Marseilles I wanted only a day from you. Now I want more. Much more. And I'm going to get it."

As they stared fixedly at one another, Ashley felt herself being taken up, absorbed into the enormous force of his will. She didn't know how to fight such a thing, or even if she wanted to. When the saleswoman returned with a selection of blouses, she sat dazed and silent while Nathan made the choice.

"This one," he said at length, holding up a long-sleeved blouse of cream-colored silk with covered buttons, a modest ruffle at each cuff, and a softly rolled collar that plunged in a deep V. "Try it on."

In the dressing room Ashley quickly slipped on the blouse and pinned the accompanying silk rose of dusty pink in the cleft of her bosom. Nathan had made a perfect decision. The blouse was feminine and flattering, yet simple enough that it did not overwhelm the rest of her ensemble. She brushed out her hair and applied fresh lipstick. The face in the mirror, with color heightened and eyes sparkling, was as pretty as she had ever seen it. It was being with him, she thought in wonder. He changed her. In spite of everything.

Nathan was waiting just outside the dressing room, arms crossed and feet planted apart. The saleswoman was talking to another customer. He raised his eyebrows. "Yes, it's perfect."

"The neckline's not too low?"

"Almost, but not quite. Decently indecent—which suits you to a T." He laughed at her puzzled expression. "Good Lord, woman, haven't you ever taken a good look at yourself? Nice but naughty—that's the impression you give. It's very provocative."

Ashley blushed. "It *is* a lovely blouse," she stammered. "I think I will take it. That is, I'll buy—" The words died on her lips. Nathan wore the same curiously pitying look that he had worn that morning in Marseilles.

"Ashley. Let me be nice to you. There's nothing to be afraid of. Examine the blouse as long as you like. You won't find any strings attached. I've had money all my life. I don't need to use it as an instrument of power in personal relationships. I only want to give you pleasure."

"But giving pleasure can be a way of gaining power over someone," Ashley parried.

"And would it be so terrible," Nathan asked, "if by giving each other pleasure, we perhaps could acquire the power to make each other happy?"

When they came out of the boutique, with Ashley wearing the blouse like a flag of surrender, their taxi was idling at the next corner. The ensuing ride was pleasant, for the tension between them had relaxed. Nathan pointed out more sights and spoke about a project at the Rome bureau of the *Report*.

Ashley said little, but her thoughts were busy. She

sensed an atmosphere of mutual yielding between them. Since she had accepted the blouse, Nathan had stopped being so aggressive and she felt less need to defend herself. His company was enjoyable, she mused. Yet there were still so many unanswered questions. What did he really want? How would it all end, and when? Nathan Trent was too busy a man to spend much time sightseeing in a city he knew well. He was also too much of a businessman not to have calculated his profit margin on the Ashley Forrester venture. So how much did he expect to gain?

As they crossed the Tiber, Nathan said, "I hope you're hungry. We're going to a working-class place in Trastevere. Simple, fresh food, and plenty of it."

To show her he wasn't trying to buy her, Ashley thought. But to him she merely said, "Sounds great. Is this another undiscovered gem?"

"Yes, an Italian reporter took me there several years ago."

"You seem to be an expert on out-of-the-way restaurants," Ashley observed.

"Show me a man who's an expert on obscure restaurants, and I'll show you a man who often dines alone— and at strange hours," Nathan returned.

"I'm sure you could have company if you wanted it. Or don't models ever eat?" Ashley teased.

He ignored the gibe. "And what about you?"

"Me? Oh, well, I don't go out much. I cook for myself."

"Are you any good?" He made his face skeptical.

"Try me and see," Ashley shot back. "Any time you're in University Park. It's the top floor of the yellow house on Maple Street."

Nathan put his hand on hers. "I haven't been to

University Park in years," he mused, "but stranger things have happened in this world." And for several minutes Ashley lost herself in a daydream of Nathan sitting in her sunny kitchen with his shoes off and his tie loosened, waiting for the chicken and dumplings bubbling on the stove. She imagined too, before she could stop herself, Nathan sprawling in the old-fashioned brass bed . . . and herself nestled beside him.

The byways of Trastevere grew steadily more narrow, crooked, and shabby, but there was a coarse vibrancy to the street life that excited Ashley. Thin men smoking dangling cigarettes played cards in the cafés. Fat women hung laundry across alleys from the upper stories of ramshackle buildings. Sooty churches huddled like forgotten grandmothers beside cobblestoned piazzas. Street vendors hawked everything from postcards to Indian bedspreads. Outside a café buzzing with tourists, a man wearing an artist's smock and a beret drew The Last Supper on the sidewalk in lurid pastels.

The Trattoria Rossini was an oasis of calm in the bustle. At Nathan's request, a waiter showed them through the crowded interior, where men in shirtsleeves and plainly dressed women eschewed conversation to concentrate on the main meal of the day, and outside to a walled patio. Under a lattice covered with flowering vines were several tables. Ashley and Nathan sat down at one of them.

When the waiter had brought bread and wine and Nathan had ordered for them both, he sat back and said, "So tell me about yourself. We hardly know each other, as the saying goes."

Ashley shrugged and broke off a piece of bread. "There's not much to tell—as another saying goes. I grew up in Cunningham, not far from University Park.

My mother died when I was two, and my father remarried two years later. The only memory I have of her—my mother, that is—is of a woman with a cloud of soft brown hair standing before a roaring fire. She has on a long red dress with sequins on the bodice." She tasted her wine. She had never told anyone about that memory. Why tell Nathan? "Or maybe it isn't my mother at all," she added hurriedly. "Maybe I'm just remembering a scene from a fairy tale."

Nathan said nothing. Stroking the flattened bridge of his nose, he listened intently. Taking confidence from his interest, Ashley rushed on. "My father traveled a lot in his business. When I was sixteen, he was killed in a car accident out in Denver. Fortunately there was enough money from the insurance to send me to college, at Creighton. During my freshman year, my stepmother remarried and moved to Arizona. I've been pretty much on my own since then. She writes once in a while and I call her on holidays."

"You've had to look out for yourself for a long time," Nathan said. "It must have been hard."

"Oh, I don't pity myself," Ashley declared. "I've done all right."

"Yes, you have," Nathan agreed, "but it's made you reluctant to accept anything from anybody."

"That's not necessarily true." But she couldn't accept his probing interest, and she half turned away.

"You know it is. And you're afraid to want anything too much. Afraid to take a risk."

"Oh? And of course you know what it is I want." This time she drank deeply.

"You want what I want. Every move you make tells me that. Your body is talking for you."

"Why is it that every conversation we have ends up

on the same subject?" she flashed.

"Because I'm a persistent man," Nathan answered with a grin. "And you're just beginning to find out how persistent." With the gesture she had already come to think of as a mark of his innate gallantry, he brought her hand to his lips and kissed the palm.

They were served tortellini—tender, ring-shaped morsels of pasta stuffed with meat—followed by a succulent veal dish and tiny artichokes. Relaxed by the first glass of wine, Ashley ate ravenously and drank two more glasses. By the time the fruit arrived, the whole world appeared to be bathed in a mellow glow. The patio, dappled by sunlight slanting through the vines, seemed to sway in a seductive dance. Ashley smiled at two matrons at the next table and at the shop owner and his assistant— or was it his young mistress?—next to them. When they smiled back, she wanted to become friends with all of them. Several tables away, an old man and a woman with a mat of hair dyed jet black argued loudly. The woman beat the table rhythmically with her fist as she ranted. The old man tried to placate her. Between slugs of wine, he patted her arm and mumbled rough endearments. When the woman burst into sobs, he began to talk louder and more rapidly. His voice rising to a fever pitch, he suddenly pulled up the cuff of his pants to reveal a wooden leg.

"*Coraggio, coraggio!*" he shouted, thumping the wood with a gnarled fist, whereupon the family at the next table all turned their chairs around and joined the altercation, without introductions.

Maudlin from the wine, Ashley's eyes filled with tears of sympathy. She wanted to join them and help with their problem. Yes, she wanted to call out, *coraggio*—take courage! "What is it all about?" she asked Nathan, and discovered that she could focus on him only with difficulty.

"Anzio. They're fighting World War II all over again." His smile floated high above her, like the Cheshire Cat's. "I think you're ready for a nap now. Anyway, it's the Roman siesta hour."

"I think I've had too much to drink," Ashley said in a voice that was not her own.

"Yes, I should have realized it wouldn't take much, considering how little you weigh." He helped her stand. As they threaded their way to the door, she found herself depending heavily on him for support. Then somehow they were in a taxi again and her head was on his shoulder.

"Everything is spinning," she breathed in awe. "Hold on to me, Nathan. Don't let go. Don't ever let me go." She threw an arm across his chest.

From miles away, he laughed softly. "I wish I had a tape recorder. You'll never admit to having said that when you sober up."

"I am sober. And I mean that," she declared, and then she was giggling, and then a long time later they were getting out of the taxi. They passed through a blur of glass doors and carved pillars and into a cool, darkly carpeted lobby. Nathan shepherded her into an elevator and helped her out several floors later, into a burgundy-toned corridor.

It wasn't until he unlocked a door and they stood in an unfamiliar room that she exclaimed, "Where are we? This isn't my room!"

"Of course not," Nathan returned, removing her shoulder bag and dropping it on a chair. "It's mine. My hotel, that is."

"But you can't—" She stared at him, bewildered.

"I mean, take me back! I want to lie down!"

"You'll lie down here." He led her farther into the room. "This is where you'll be staying. I've had your luggage sent over."

And indeed, there they were—her two suitcases and portable typewriter.

"Nathan Trent! You had no right!" Ashley yelled. "I'm not staying here another second!" She started for her luggage, but in her condition it was an easy matter for Nathan to catch her and spin her around.

"Just calm down and listen to me," he said in a low voice, his hands spanning her waist. "This is not my room. My room is through that connecting door. I'm giving you the key to it." Freeing one hand, he brought a key out of his pocket and tossed it on a table.

Their faces were inches apart. Ashley felt his breath coming irregularly, stirring the wisps of hair at her temples. "I don't understand. I want to go back to my own room," she protested weakly, her voice looping crazily.

"I have work to do in Rome and so do you," Nathan explained. "I'm not going to interfere with that. And I'm not forcing you into anything. But I want you, darling, more all the time. And I want you here, next to me, until you realize that you feel the same way. That's what this is all about." Gently he leaned down and kissed her. "Besides, your other room has already been rented."

His kisses made her go all soft inside, until everything had dissolved into a light, hollow ache. Winding her arms around his neck, she pressed her hips into him and felt him respond. "I want you now," she whispered thickly. "I do." She pulled his head down until his lips grazed the upper roundness of her breasts. "Now," she pleaded, kissing his hair.

"No." His voice was hoarse, tortured. "Not when

you're like this. Not when you don't know what you're doing. I want all of you at once."

Dizzily she was aware that he was carrying her, and then that she was lying on her back on a bed. He slipped off her shoes. "Nathan, please—" She tried to sit up but he pushed her back. "But my new blouse! I'll get it wrinkled!" That seemed very important.

He sat down on the edge of the bed. "Just the rose. I'll take it off." And his fingers fumbled between her breasts, trembling slightly. Then the rose came away and her breasts seemed suddenly to ripen and swell together. Ashley sighed and closed her eyes. The room kept spinning, but she felt deliciously comfortable. Spreading her arms and legs wide, she stretched luxuriantly and felt the top button of the blouse come undone.

The mattress dipped as Nathan's weight shifted toward her. "My God," he said huskily, "if you ever tempt me like this again—"

The last thing she remembered was the weight of his chest pressing her down...and the firm, demanding warmth of his mouth on hers.

chapter 7

THE HAMMER HIT the coconut with a crack. The coconut groaned. The hammer descended again, rattling the shell with the blow. A hairline split snaked across the shell.

Ashley rolled over and sat up holding her head, which in her dream had been the coconut. She had a crashing headache. Her throat was dry and her tongue felt like a wad of cotton. Hangover, she understood dimly, and squinted as another stabbing pain hit.

Her eyes flew open. Nathan, had—? She was fully dressed except for her shoes and a button open at the top of her blouse. So they must not have . . . She touched her lips gingerly with her fingertips. Puffy and a little raw. From him. She took up the rose and the key from the bedside table and turned them over in her hands. Nathan. From the next room she heard a drawer opening, papers shuffling, his voice, a telephone receiver being replaced. He was working.

Stiffly she got off the bed and went to the window. The twilit city, bejeweled and vastly wistful, greeted her. She switched on lights and explored the room. Connected both to her room and Nathan's was a bathroom spectacular in black tile, with a wide, sunken tub. It would be like bathing in a private pool, she reflected, and a hot, steaming soak was just what she needed. What a change from the pensione's one bathroom per floor! Impulsively she turned on the taps full blast and locked the door to Nathan's room. Then she quickly pinned her hair on top of her head, shook a few drops of bath oil into the water, and stripped off her clothes. As she slid into the water, she heard him moving about near the door, pacing as he talked again on the phone, and she felt strangely stirred to have him so near and yet oblivious to her nakedness. She lay back, letting the heat soothe her.

Maybe this was all one should expect of life, anyway—a brief idyll now and then, a few unforgettable weeks sprinkled over the years. Maybe she was wrong—or at least naive—to insist on anything more. It would be so much easier just to give in to Nathan, to let him enjoy her and to enjoy him as long as he would let her. She pressed the heels of her hands hard into her aching temples. It was too difficult to know what to do. But at least she ought to stop fighting him long enough to give him a chance to see her best side.

Raising one slender leg from the water, she examined the bruise on her knee. But if they did have an affair, how could she ever go back to her sedate life in University Park, or anywhere else? How, even now, could she ever get over him? He had already ruined her for anyone else. She sighed and began to lather herself with soap that smelled of sandalwood.

The moment she returned to her room, wrapped in an enormous, fluffy towel and with her bones soft as jelly from the moist heat, there was a knock at the connecting door.

"Just a minute—two minutes!" she called gaily, for she had made up her mind to unbend a little and see what happened. Moving swiftly but with care, because of her headache, she slipped on a lacy camisole and panties, then a sleeveless blue jersey dress that matched her eyes. Wiggling her toes into the bone sling-backed heels she had bought in Marseilles, she hurried to open the door.

Nathan strode in carrying a tray. "I ordered coffee."

He grinned. "Thought you might need it. How do you feel?"

He put the tray on a table by the window overlooking the city, then he flung himself onto one of the two chairs flanking it. He was wearing his horn-rimmed glasses. His tie was off and his shirtsleeves were rolled up.

"My head feels wretched, but the rest of me will live," Ashley told him, unpinning her hair so that it tumbled around her shoulders. She sat down and took the cup he filled for her, waving away cream and sugar with a shudder.

With a twinkle, Nathan took a tin of aspirins from his shirt pocket and shook two out in his palm. Handing them over, he said, *"In vino veritas:* in wine there is truth. Do you remember anything of what you said?"

"No. Yes. Well, some."

"I had to fight for my virtue, you know. In this very room." He added sugar to his cup and stirred. "I barely escaped."

"Oh, Nathan!" She reddened.

He leaned back nonchalantly, his fingers laced behind his head. "I got to see the real Ashley for a change, and let me tell you, she's something else. A tigress, maybe."

Her blush deepened as she started to remember. "I'm sorry. I shouldn't have had that last glass of wine. It's just that I was enjoying myself so much—"

"Sorry? Don't be sorry. I'm not. I was beginning to think I wasn't having any effect on you at all." He reached out a hand and caressed her cheek with lazy satisfaction.

"I think you planned the whole thing just to get me moved in this room without a fight," Ashley charged.

"It did make things easier," he agreed, "but I can't take credit for planning it." He pushed his glasses up on his forehead and rubbed his eyes. "I hope we're not going to fight that battle now."

"Not at all," Ashley returned levelly. "It's a nice room. I'd like to stay."

"Well, well." He raised his eyebrows. "You leave me speechless. I didn't expect such cooperation."

"I said I liked the room. I didn't say anything about cooperation." She was pleased to see uncertainty on his face for a change. But he quickly resumed command.

"Ah." He emptied his coffee cup. "Well, it looks like I have my work cut out for me, Miss Forrester, if I intend to seduce you. Shall we go?"

"Where?"

"How about a moonlight ride through Rome in a horse-drawn carriage? It's a romantic thing to do." He stood over her, half mocking and half serious.

"Mr. Trent," Ashley said coolly, "I think I'm beginning to like your style."

And it *was* romantic. Keeping to dark, less-traveled streets and occasionally surfacing amid bright lights around the Piazza Navona, where the sidewalk cafés were humming, or before the half-lit Pantheon, they wound slowly through the city. Above the open carriage the constellations sparkled. Below it, the clip-clop of the horse's hooves and the bump of the wheels over uneven pavement sang a choppy tune. Inside, Nathan put his arm around Ashley to protect her from the chill, and she snuggled against him. Once, when she sighed deeply, he asked why.

"I keep expecting the coach to turn back into a pumpkin, I guess," she answered softly.

He tilted her chin up so that she had to look at him. "And would you be sorry?"

"Yes, Nathan. Yes, I would."

The ghost of a frown flitted across his face, almost as if he had experienced a sudden pain. "Hmmmmm," he said, gathering her closer to him, "I'll see what I can do about the problem."

She was glad that the dark hid her consternation. Where were they going? she asked herself in desperation. Where were they *really* going?

It was very late when Nathan paid the driver and they took a narrow stairway two flights up to a rooftop restaurant called Alfredo's.

"Shall I order for you?" he asked. They were seated at a table bearing a fresh carnation in a bud vase and a burning candle in a silver candlestick.

"Yes," she said, "but nothing much. And no wine, for heaven's sake!"

"A small steak, then. They're very good here—Florentine steaks cooked over olive wood. And mineral water?" He took her hand across the table and pressed it. His eyes, dark and liquid with contentment, fondled her face.

Ashley wanted to weep for happiness. It was a dream come true—the carriage ride, the intimate surroundings, sitting across from the man she was falling in love with, listening to a pleasantly jaded redhead sing about love. For even though the song was in Italian, anyone could tell that the subject was love. Could such a lush woman sing of anything else? For a few moments, as Ashley absently stroked Nathan's long, strong fingers, she was in a daze. Yes, somehow she'd fallen in love with him. No matter what he was up to, damn it. But as soon as the thought crossed her mind, she felt Nathan's hand tense imperceptibly.

The singer stood across the room from them, leaning back on the piano that accompanied her. Her voice was low and throaty; the bodice of her strapless gown was even lower. As she sang, she moved in a slow, sensuous rhythm against the curve of the wood. There was something purposely and personally provocative about her performance, as if she were singing not to an audience but to one person only. And as Ashley followed the direction of Nathan's gaze, and saw how he and the singer were eyeing each other, she had a sinking feeling that she knew who that one person was.

It was like rubbing salt in a wound to ask, "Do you know her?"

Reluctantly, it seemed, he tore his eyes away. "What? Yes, that's Dominique." He paused. "I didn't know she was singing here tonight."

"I'll bet you didn't."

"What's that supposed to mean?" he growled.

"This morning we paraded past Renata, who just happens to be in Rome at the same time you are. Now we're to be entertained by another of your lady friends, who just happens to be singing in the restaurant you picked. Small world, isn't it?" She sat back with folded arms. For Dominique had stepped off the small stage and was singing her way toward them.

She was about Ashley's height but more curvaceous. The shimmering green material of her long dress clung to her like a second skin and magnified every sinuous motion as she progressed through the diners, stopping at a table here and there to sing a phrase but never turning from her path. When she sat down in Nathan's lap and finished her song with her arm around his neck and her cheek against his, appreciative laughter and applause broke out.

"Hello, Dominique," Nathan said with a cryptic smile. "Better be careful about being so friendly with the guests.

You know Alfredo doesn't like it."

"But when it's you, Nathan!" She looked over her well-rounded shoulder at Ashley. "You know he'll understand."

Ashley went through the motions of being introduced, but all she was aware of was the way Nathan's hand rested on Dominique's waist. There was an unconscious ease about it that suggested long practice.

"I was expecting you, of course," Dominique informed him. "Just yesterday I said to myself, 'It's about time for Nathan to show up again, on his monthly trip to Rome.'" She turned heavily made-up eyes on Ashley. "New secretary?"

"No," Nathan responded, finally having the decency to look uncomfortable. "A friend."

Ashley felt sick. A friend. Well, he was right. They were just friends, if that. Heaven only knew what Dominique was.

The waiter arrived with their steaks. With a peck on the mouth for Nathan, Dominique stood up and smoothed her dress over her hips. "I have to finish my show. I'll see you later." Half turned away from Ashley, she mouthed to Nathan, And you know where. *"Ciao,"* she told Ashley.

"Dominique is . . . impulsive," Nathan said indifferently, cutting into his steak.

"And so am I. Take me home." Ashley threw down her napkin.

"What a little homebody you are. You're always wanting to go home." He took a bite of steak. "Excellent. Try it."

"Then I'll find my own way!" Ashley rose too fast and knocked the table sideways. Nathan caught it at the edge to keep it from turning over, and in the ensuing clatter of china and silver, everyone looked at them.

"Sit down," he said tightly.

Mortified, Ashley did as she was told. For several minutes neither one of them spoke. Ashley knew that Nathan was furious with her for making a scene, yet she felt it was unfair of him to put her in the wrong. As she watched him devour the steak, while she herself could not swallow a bite, she grew increasingly nettled. Finally she exploded.

"How do you expect me to feel? You should have explained about Dominique!"

"There's nothing to explain."

"You mean there's nothing you care to explain! I can read lips, you know. She's pretty sure of herself."

Very carefully Nathan set down his glass. Then from the center of the table he picked up the candle and blew on it so that the flame flickered. "That's what the beginning of a relationship between a man and a woman is like," he said, looking at her steadily across the dancing blaze. "A candle in the wind. Almost anything can extinguish it—the merest breeze, a single word. It takes a lot of patience to keep it burning, and I'm beginning to lose mine. In fact, I'm beginning to think I made a mistake."

"What kind of mistake?"

"I think," Nathan said, "that I shouldn't have tried to light anything between us. You'll use any excuse to blow it out."

"How dare you put me on the defensive again!" Ashley stormed. "Nobody sat down in my lap! And we haven't even discussed what Renata is doing here. I refuse to take the blame!"

Without another word, Nathan closed thumb and forefinger around the candle flame and pinched the wick until it went out. He gave no indication that he felt the fire at all. Throwing down some bills without counting them, he pushed back his chair.

"Let's go. I'm tired of this."

In the taxi, all the way back to the hotel, Ashley kept her face turned to the window and fought off tears. Was it over between them, and for so small a thing? Was he right? Was it impossible for them to get along? Was she supposed to never question him, as she had never questioned Clay until it was too late? And what had Dominique meant by mentioning Nathan's secretary? Was she, Ashley, only taking the place of his secretary for this one trip?

When they stepped out of the elevator on their floor, Nathan went to his room without speaking to her. And Ashley, without undressing, threw herself across her bed and cried herself to sleep. She awoke once, when she heard Nathan go out. She never heard him come back.

chapter 8

THE NEXT MORNING, Ashley was at the door of the hotel dining room when it opened for breakfast. Wishing neither to be in the room when Nathan returned nor to be disappointed if he didn't, she sat at her table for hours, drinking the rich, gritty Italian coffee and writing up a story for the *Chronicle*. For the first time since she had begun her trip, she was embarrassed to be sitting alone. Every time someone crossed the threshold, she looked up, but it was never he. Finally, when the morning was well along, she bought a new guidebook and caught a bus to Vatican City. Leaving St. Peter's Basilica for another day, she plunged into the welter of Vatican museums. The contemplation of great works of art had always been a way of escape for her.

Not that day. Raphael's paintings went by like so many movie posters. The *Apollo Belvedere,* though too finely wrought, reminded her of Nathan, and the writhing Laocoön sculpture, in which the serpent sent by Apollo crushes the priest and his sons, seemed to represent her own torment. Only during the time she spent in the Sistine Chapel, gazing wonder-struck at Michelangelo's ceiling and altar wall, did she succeed in losing herself.

In mid-afternoon, as she stood on a packed, suffocating bus going back to the hotel, she went over Nathan's conduct in Rome from beginning to end and found little to reproach him for. He had taken the trouble to find her. He had wined and dined her and had provided a beautiful room for her stay. Yet he hadn't forced him-

self on her as he had in Marseilles. He had only suc-
cumbed, as had she, to the mutual attraction that crackled
between them.

She stepped off the bus and walked a block to the
hotel. His affairs with Dominique and Renata might already be over, she reasoned, although she was all too
aware of the desperation in her argument. In fact, Dominique might be nothing more than a flirtatious acquaintance. But where had he spent last night? a small
voice cried. Furthermore, she had no real proof that he
was carrying on a contest with Clay. Ask him. Why
didn't she ask him?

Motive, she thought, as she reached her room and
went straight to her typewriter. It all boiled down to what
his motives were. She would have to ask him, but carefully. The last thing she wanted was to drive him into
someone else's arms. Or had she already done that?

An hour and a half later, when she heard his door
open, her fingers went limp on the keys. This was it.
Taking a deep breath, she gathered up the story she had
been typing and went to the connecting door. With her
hand raised to knock, however, she took fright and re-
treated a few steps. In the dresser mirror she caught a
glimpse of a medium-tall figure with slender legs and
waist, full breasts, and hips wide enough to balance them.
"You're nicely shaped for childbearing," was how her
stepmother had put it. Ashley was generally comfortable
enough with her appearance, but now she saw that she
was too quiet-looking for Nathan, if models and enter-
tainers were what he liked. But she tossed back her hair,
squared her shoulders, and with a last, worried look at
the glass, rapped on the panel.

Nathan jerked open the door, still holding the sports
coat he had just removed. He looked her up and down,
his eyes wary. "Well?"

Ashley licked her lips. "I was wondering if you'd give me your opinion on what I've just written. I'm not sure it's right."

"Sure." He was noncommital. "Come on in." He took the pages from her, ambled over to a paper-strewn desk, and sat down. "Make yourself at home."

Unnerved by his composure, Ashley found it impossible to keep still. She roamed from one end of the room to the other, running her fingers over the furniture and whistling tunelessly between her teeth. A pair of cuff links on the dresser caught her attention momentarily. Of monogrammed brushed gold, they were not the sort of thing a man would buy for himself. She had once purchased Clay a monogrammed tie clasp that could have been part of the same set.

Nathan hunched forward in total concentration, a stubborn set to his shoulders and neck. Nathan Trent, the formidable publisher, poring over her work! She half expected him to fling it back in her face.

"Come here," he commanded at last, throwing down his pencil. Ashley went to stand behind him. "These two paragraphs here. You should reverse their order. And then down here, cut this sentence, since the information is already given in paragraph one." He handed the pages back, over his shoulder. "Okay?"

"That's all?" she asked meekly.

"Yep. It's a good story. If you weren't already working for me, I'd hire you." He opened a folder and took up his pencil again. The silence in the room grew.

"Well, thank you," Ashley said to the back of his neck. It was no use. She didn't have the courage to confront him. She turned to go.

The light from the desk lamp flashed on Nathan's jaw as he clenched and unclenched it. He swung his chair around. "Ashley, I—" He ran a hand through his hair.

"I'm sorry Dominique embarrassed you. Believe me, I didn't know she'd be there."

Ashley looked down at the carpet, terrified that she would cry. "I apologize for making a scene. But I don't understand how I fit in your life. There are so many others, aren't there?"

"There have been, over the years. You can't expect me to change my past. Anyway, it has nothing to do with you."

"My stepmother used to say, 'Never expect a man to change for you. Take him the way he is or leave him alone,'" Ashley ventured. "You know how I am. I'm not the sort to take a number and wait in line. I really think I should stay somewhere else. I shouldn't have accepted the room in the first place."

With a bearlike sweep of his arm, Nathan pulled her into his lap. He scrutinized her face solemnly. All at once he smiled, and it was like the sun breaking through the clouds. "You little fool." He kissed her on the nose. "Can't you see how crazy I am about you? What else do I have to do to prove it? If you hadn't found a pretext to come to me, I would have come to you." He shook his head in good-natured exasperation.

"But last night...I thought it was over." She toyed with a button on his shirt, avoiding his eyes. "Wasn't that what you meant by snuffing out the candle?"

"So I'll buy some matches. It doesn't have to be over." He shifted his thighs so that she slid against his chest. "I'm just getting damned tired of trying to figure out how to please you."

"Please me?" Ashley put her arms around his neck. "Oh, Nathan, if you only knew—"

They stared at each other, feeling everything start all over again. Then Nathan kissed her eyes, her cheeks, her mouth, slowly exploring her skin. He kissed her chin and her throat, his breath sending delicious shivers down the length of her body. She closed her eyes. Twining her fingers in his hair, she held him to her, letting the warm, feathery kisses on her throat unlock one door after another in her resistance. When he buried his face between her breasts, she caught her breath in a little sigh and bowed her head over his.

"Can't you feel it?" he whispered. "How much we belong together? How your body keeps calling to mine?"

"Yes, yes." The words were torn from her, against her will . . . and not.

And then, with her in his arms, he stood and crossed the room. As he put her down on the bed and sat on the edge, leaning over her while his hand stroked the curve of her hip, a dim memory of the questions she wanted to ask floated past. But when he stretched out beside her and gathered her to him, a new, sharp hunger for him drove away everything else. Locked in each other's arms, they tussled playfully, rolling over and over. His kisses were more urgent now, demanding more and more as her body melted in a slow fire, readying itself to give. As wave after wave of new sensations flamed through her, she thought: it had never been like this. She'd never known it could be. . . .

"Missed you today," he murmured. "I hope you don't have anything planned for tonight." He raised himself on one elbow. A mischievous gleam in his eye, he traced a line with his finger from the hollow of her throat down her breastbone, stopping to circle each breast. As they peaked with pleasure, he grinned wickedly. "Or tomorrow night. Or the next night."

She couldn't answer, so mesmerized was she by the nearness of his eyes, the lids iridescent and heavy with desire, the sensual mouth, the savagely broken nose. As they rolled over again, their legs intertwined, driving his hard, muscled thigh between hers and molding them into one single need. As his lips punished hers, Ashley moaned softly in anticipation. Yet still there was one small part of her that held out, one part that would not let her surrender completely until she *knew*.

"Nathan," she gasped, tearing her mouth from his, "I have to know something."

"No talking." He kissed her shoulder and pulled gently at her ear lobe with his teeth. "Talk later."

"Wait. I have to ask," she insisted. "You called the *Chronicle*. To find out where I was."

"Mmmm."

"You talked to Clay?"

"Mmmm."

"Did you?"

His weight shifted slightly. "Yeah, I did. Sit up, honey," he coaxed, raising her shoulders. "Let me undress you."

Ashley sat up and twisted away from him. "Is this the way you usually avoid discussions?"

"I didn't know we were having a discussion. I thought we were doing something else entirely." A dangerous note of anger had crept into his voice.

"What did you talk about with Clay?" She withdrew farther from him.

"This is neither the time nor the place." He put a hand around her waist and pulled her roughly back.

"It is precisely the right time and place." She pushed his hand away. "What did you say to each other? Did you tell him it was your turn with me now?"

"He had his chance and he blew it. He admits that. And he's not going to get another one." He scowled at her, all tenderness forgotten.

"Did you make a bet?" she spat out.

"Clay doesn't bet when the odds are this much against him," Nathan drawled, reaching for her again.

"Are you going to telephone him the minute we finish making love and tell him the new score? What do you get, a loving cup?" Nathan moved toward her, but she scrambled off the other side of the bed, trembling with anger. "Please answer me!"

His chest heaved with the effort of controlling himself. "You're pathologically suspicious, do you know that? And incapable, it seems, of forgetting about one man when you're in the arms of another!"

"Oh, listen to this," Ashley jeered. "From you, who have the morals of a fox in a henhouse! How can I trust you?" As the tears spilled down her cheeks, she turned and ran to her room, locking the door behind her.

It was not long before she heard Nathan's door slam as he left. For the rest of the miserable day, she telephoned hotel after hotel, but between the tourist season at its height and the limits of her Italian, she could not find another room. She tried to write but was too nervous. In early evening she went downstairs for a sandwich, stopping by the registration desk on her way to the dining room.

"I'd like to change rooms," she told the clerk.

"You are not satisfied with your present room?" he inquired with haughty surprise.

"No, I'm not. That is, the room itself is fine, but—" Her cheeks flamed. "I'd just like another room, please. On another floor. A single."

"And what is your room number?"

She told him, then watched in humiliation as he looked up the number and discovered that she was the other party with Nathan Trent. The clerk made a show of checking the guest register, but Ashley already knew what the answer would be before he folded his hands and said, "I'm sorry, but we have nothing else."

"Are you sure? I'll take anything. It's important." She gripped the edge of the counter.

The clerk shook his head—with a certain satisfaction, she imagined. "We have a steady clientele. Many of the rooms are held for our frequent guests."

"Then I'll be settling my bill soon. How much is my room per day?" she asked.

The clerk permitted himself a raised eyebrow. "It's been put on Mr. Trent's bill."

"Then take it off."

But when he told her the price, she gasped in astonishment. It would take nearly every cent she had. But pay it she would, even if it meant flying home early. She had lost all interest in the trip, anyway.

"Thank you," she managed to say. "As soon as I know my plans, I'll be checking out."

She went on to the dining room, but ate little. Like a rat in a maze, her mind ran distractedly in all directions, seeking escape from her intolerable situation. As soon as she was back in her room, she climbed into bed and entered a deep, dreamless sleep that lasted well into the next morning.

The instant she awakened, she knew that one of the reasons she had slept so heavily was that there had been no sound from the other room. Nathan, it seemed, had another bed somewhere in Rome. And all the hotels were full. . . .

An hour later, in the airlines office, she regarded the woman behind the computer with dismay. "Not until tomorrow? But I have to get home. Aren't there any night flights? Or how about standby? I can go out to the airport and wait."

"We do not advise it," the woman said in stilted English. "At this time of year there are so many students waiting for a flight. They sleep in the airport with their backpacks." She punched some buttons. "Very fortunately, we have just had a cancellation for tomorrow afternoon, as I said. But that is all."

"Oh, all right, if that's the best you can do," Ashley said petulantly, then caught herself. "I'm sorry. I know it's not your fault. It's just that I've...I've had some bad news."

Thirty hours, she said as she walked aimlessly. Thirty hours to kill. Then she could go home and let Clay laugh at her.

The summer sun had turned the city into an oven. At length, finding herself outside the gates to the Borghese Gardens, which were on her list of things to see, Ashley decided to seek relief in the art gallery in the Villa Borghese.

But she had never felt so uncomfortable and depressed as she did strolling alone through the cool marble interior, past wall after wall of paintings she could not enjoy. Over and over she asked herself, what was to become of her? Was it her or was it men? Why did she let herself in for such failures? Oblivious to her surroundings, she was agonizing over these questions when she heard a woman's voice say, "I don't get it. There must be a legend behind it. Does your book tell what it's about, Miss?"

Ashley came back from her preoccupations with a start. She was standing before the famous statue of Apollo and Daphne, and two American women were waiting for her answer.

"Why, yes," she stammered, "I read about it before I came." She looked up at the youthful figure of the nymph Daphne, who twists away from the pursuing god Apollo. "You see, Apollo is in love with Daphne because Cupid has shot him with an arrow of love. But Daphne is running away because Cupid shot *her* with an arrow of fear and hate. Just as Apollo is about to catch her, she calls on her father, a river god, to save her. He changes her into a laurel tree, and that's what you see here." All three studied the figure of Daphne, whose hair was turning to leaves, whose toes were growing roots, and whose nude body was half sheathed in bark. As the women thanked her and wandered off, Ashley mused. She was just like Daphne. Always afraid, always running. Even when she was engaged. And gradually she was turning into something fleshless and bloodless to protect herself. Just like poor Daphne. She turned on her heel. But what else could she do? Her Apollo didn't love her.

She walked all afternoon. By the time she got back to the hotel, wilted and footsore, all she could think of was a long bath. Throwing off her clothes and barely pausing for her robe, she hurried to the sunken tub and was soon lolling in water up to her neck. Resting her head against the edge, she closed her eyes and made her mind go blank. Once she wondered if she would see Nathan before her departure, now less than twenty-four hours away, but she was too exhausted to pursue the thought. After a while, just as the water was growing tepid, she heard a key turn in the lock of her room.

She sat up to listen. Footsteps, and then a noise like something heavy being set down. Perhaps it was the maid, bringing a box of cleaning supplies or fresh linen. Had the bed been made? She couldn't remember. She slid back down in the water, still alert. The footsteps, muffled by the carpet, were hard to follow, but they seemed to be going all around the room. She heard the drapes being adjusted. Yes, the maid was straightening up. Late in the day for that, though. Satisfied, Ashley added more hot water and went on soaking. Later she noticed that the noises had stopped. When the water cooled again, she got out of the tub and toweled herself off without haste. She felt lightheaded and remembered that she had forgotten about lunch, but the bath had rested and refreshed her. Humming to herself, she slipped on the turquoise kimono, belted it, and opened the door to her room.

She stopped on the threshold, unable to believe what she saw.

The drapes had been closed, so that the room should have been dark. But a cluster of candles burned on the bedside table. Burning candles covered the entire surfaces of the dresser and the window table. There were candles everywhere, tall and short, thick and thin, bright and dim—more candles than she had ever seen in her life. The air was heavy with the scent of melting wax. In a chair by the window, a glass of whiskey in his hand, sat Nathan. He was looking at her with an intensity that burned brighter than all the candles in the world.

chapter 9

NATHAN SWIRLED THE ice in his glass. Without taking his eyes off her, he finished the drink in one swallow and set the tumbler down among the candles at his elbow. He stretched out his legs and crossed them at the ankles. He wore tight-fitting white slacks and a light-blue shirt open at the neck, and he was barefoot. He had recently showered and shaved. In the candlelight, his still-damp curls glistened like finely carved ebony.

Ashley ventured a few steps into the room and stopped, uncertain how to proceed. It was her room no longer, if it had ever been. She had entered another realm—unreal, uncertain in the wavering glow, and Nathan's. Her heart beat heavily, like a slow drum.

"Sit down."

She took the chair opposite his and concentrated on her toes. It was so still that she could hear the candles burning. She coughed nervously.

"I hear you're checking out."

"News travels fast." It came out a whisper.

"Going back to University Park?"

Ashley fingered the sash of her kimono. "I don't know what else to do." She could feel his eyes wandering over her with the soft, deliberate pressure of a cat's paws. She coughed again.

"I do."

She jerked her head up. "Do what?"

"I know what else you can do. There's an alternative." But his voice was not kind. It had a harsh, matter-of-fact ring to it. "I thought of it last night."

"Wherever you were."

"Does it matter?"

Briefly she considered not answering. But it did matter. More than he would ever know. "Yes. Unfortunately for me, it does."

He let that ride for a while. Then he said easily, "Dominique and I have known each other for years. We once spent a week in Greece together, but that was long ago, when I was very young and any woman three years older than I seemed infinitely desirable. Now she's married to Alfredo, the owner of the restaurant. He used to be the food editor of a magazine I owned, and usually we all get together when I'm in Rome. He was busy in the kitchen the other night, as the waiter informed me and as I neglected to translate for you. If we hadn't left so soon, he would have joined us."

"But she said—"

"Oh, I know what Dominique said," Nathan cut in. "She's a great tease. I knew the minute I saw her that she would do or say something crazy. And I would have warned you if I'd known she would be there. Especially if I'd had any idea you would react as you did," he added pointedly. "Still, I'm surprised she went quite that far." He shrugged to dismiss the subject.

He was not apologetic. He was not trying to persuade her of anything. Yet she sensed that it was a difficult exchange for him. He was not used to justifying his actions.

"I guess I jumped to conclusions," she confessed.

"That you did."

The candles, now burning at their zenith, painted the room with enchantment and tipped Nathan's temples, cheekbones, and the sinews of his hands with gold. Ashley shifted in her chair and the panels of the kimono separated, uncovering one gilded leg to the thigh.

"I don't know what to say," she offered. She was touched by his willingness to explain, but she had not forgotten that he owed her the explanation.

"As for Renata," Nathan resumed, "she is only a bauble."

Ashley raised her eyebrows. "That's not a very nice thing to say about someone."

"It's pretty charitable, considering how she thinks of me." He sat forward, elbows on knees, and continued with weary amusement. "Renata doesn't have many years of modeling left, and she has few other talents. When she looks at me, she sees one thing—money. The money to keep her for the rest of her life in the manner to which I have accustomed her." He waved a hand and said, self-mockingly, "One of the disadvantages of wealth."

"Poor little rich boy."

"But the greater advantage of the situation is this—Renata and I understand each other perfectly. Neither one of us has labored under any illusion about what we mean to each other."

"An equal exchange of goods and services. I'm so happy for you." Ashley left her chair and began to roam, hugging herself as if her body were as cold as her words. In fact, she was trying to control the physical tension that threatened to break out into trembling at any moment. Stopping beside a bank of candles, she stared down at them, unseeing. The old ache for him throbbed inside her. At the same time, his cool, calculating control terrified her. On the one hand he seemed to be settling his account with her, closing the books. But on the other, there were the candles, and the message from him that they seemed to be whispering, must be whispering—

She jumped as his arms went around her from behind.

"Now then," he said against her ear, "let's talk about you."

She watched a flame change from yellow to blue to orange and back again. "What about me?"

"Oh, about what a royal pain you are. About everything I left undone in Marseilles to chase after you, only to have you suspect me of ulterior motives. About how you can't be bought—" he chuckled "—or even rented, and how I respect you for it. About the way you're running back to University Park like a singed puppy. About the crick I've got in my neck from sleeping on the couch in my office—"

Without breaking the circle of his arms, Ashley whirled to face him. "That's where you were?"

"Sure," he said gruffly. "Does it matter?"

"It means the world to me," she said shyly.

He tried to scowl, but good humor danced in the lines around his mouth. "You know, I said I could give you an alternative to going back home. Actually, there is none. Or rather, you've left *me* no alternative. There's only one way to convince you that I'm serious and at the same time get my life back on schedule." With one hand he caught her mane of hair at the nape of her neck and, gently but with unmistakable firmness, held her head motionless so that she was forced to confront his stormy countenance. They never strayed far from that, she reflected—from the awareness of his superior strength and his readiness to use it. "This is no candle in the wind, Ashley. The fire has spread." He nodded toward a forest of burning tapers across the room. "I'm in love with you."

"I know. I know that now." Like a cold mist, the nervous strain she had been under for days lifted, leaving in its place an enormous, bone-bending relief. She collapsed against him and was wetting his shirt with hot tears of happiness when he spoke again.

"You're not leaving. I want to marry you. Soon. Before anything can separate us again."

"Nothing ever can." She smiled as he took her face in his hands and wiped away the tears one at a time. "Not ever again. I love you so much."

Holding her by the hand, Nathan led her back to his chair by the window. He sat down and hauled her into his lap, where she curled up like a kitten.

"This is where you belong," he said, and planted a full-lipped kiss on each of her eyelids and on her mouth to seal the promise.

In the magical light they talked for hours. "I have been married before," Nathan said after a time. "Did you know that?"

Ashley raised her head from his shoulder. "Charles LeSueur told me a little. I'm sorry, so sorry about the accident. What you must have gone through, losing someone you love just at the start of your life together. It's hard for me to imagine how you came through it."

"You're nothing like Ingrid. I want you to know that," Nathan said gravely. Ashley couldn't help recoiling slightly at his words, and he tightened his embrace. "Wait a minute. Let me explain. After the accident in Switzerland and Ingrid's death, I went through several stages. Everyone goes through them in such situations—denial, anger, depression, and finally, if one perseveres, acceptance of what has happened. At first I didn't care whether I recovered or not, and I did very little to help the doctors with their job. Later on, when I was strong again, I spent some years on useless pleasures, trying to erase the memories. Still later, there was the tendency to idealize Ingrid and to search for another just like her. But I've worked through all of that. I want you to understand and never to doubt that I love you for yourself and for no other reason."

"I want to give you a new beginning," Ashley whispered, stroking his cheek. "That's what you've given me."

When it was quite dark Nathan ordered dinner, and they ate looking down on the nocturnal city. Afterward, when the dishes had been removed, he collected all the big pillar candles that were still burning and grouped them on the table beside the bed.

Ashley sat watching him prowl the room like a great cat. His shirt was open to the waist, for she had unbuttoned it as they talked, and the sight of the light playing over his body made her pulse go shallow and quick. She waited, knowing what she was waiting for.

Nathan finished his task. Now all of the light in the room was focused on the bed. He came to stand in front of her. Flames leaped in his eyes and his enormous shadow fell across her with a force she could almost feel. Slowly he stripped off his shirt and dropped it behind him. Then he took her hands and gently raised her to her feet.

His eyes locked with hers as his fingers found the knot of her sash and untied it. With a smile he tore the sash away and tossed it onto his shirt. Then he opened her kimono, and she heard a sharp intake of breath as the light struck her naked body. The next moment the robe slid from her shoulders and fell in a blue pool at her feet.

For an instant only she had the sensation of being outside her body and looking down on a golden figurine, whose curves were polished into fullness by the candlelight. Then Nathan touched her and she became flesh, all flesh, again. His hands took hold of her at the hips and pulled her to him. As she looked down at the pinkness of her breasts riding on his dark chest hair, his hands slid around to her buttocks and drew her hard against him, so that her nails dug into his shoulders with the pleasurable shock. The kiss that followed reached to the roots of her being, and she understood wildly that nothing could be held back from a man like this, a man who knew so strongly what he wanted and knew how to get it and would never stop until he owned all of her.

They sank down on the bed together, his lips teasing her nipples with soft nipping kisses, her hands moving over him in ways she had never been taught and had never thought of before. When she stroked the length of his thighs, their strength and hardness stirred her unbearably.

With a groan Nathan pulled himself away to finish undressing. "I think," he said with a crooked grin, "that you have a talent for this."

She smiled and rolled onto her side to watch him, propping an elbow on the pillows. She had never felt so comfortable with her own body, or so ready to enjoy the mysteries of love. Her senses were alive to his every movement.

"Why did you go on in such a mercenary relationship with Renata?" she asked idly. "You could have any woman."

He returned, now unclothed, to the edge of the bed. "I never wanted any woman. Until now."

He knelt over her, and Ashley ran her hand down the matted hair on his chest . . . down his hard, flat belly . . . down to the cruel white scars that lashed his right leg. Touching him, she felt like the new queen of a vast and magnificent country, and her impatience to take possession of it made her warm and giddy. When he lay down beside her and his evenly muscled body came into firm contact with hers, she stiffened with a flowering of desire so intense that it was almost painful.

But he wanted to explore her first. As his kisses, sweet like wine and sharp like salt, probed deeper and deeper into her need for him, she lay back and let him discover her slowly and exquisitely, not as a country is conquered but as the center of a rosebud is laid bare by tearing away the petals one by one. And finally she could not remain passive, could not wait any longer to feel his weight upon her. She wrapped her arms around him and rolled onto her back. For a moment his face was suspended above her, bronzed with the intensity of his passion, before his lips dipped suddenly to her neck, and at the same time his knee forced her legs apart. Her body rose to meet his and they flowed together in a rhythm that built and built as if it would never stop, a rhythm that carried her soaring higher than she had ever dreamed was possible, until at last it broke with rapture.

Long after the last candle had guttered out and dawn whispered at the window, she lay still awake, treasuring a contentment too precious to lose in sleep. Snuggled against him, her arm thrown across his chest, she mused on the plans they had made. From time to time she raised herself to scan his sleeping face, where now the stern lines had softened and the real sensitivity of the man showed through. Once Nathan awakened with a start and sat up, but when he saw her there, he smiled sleepily and lay back down, curled around her. That was the way she finally fell asleep, with her head cradled on his out-flung arm.

The aromas of coffee and aftershave woke her some hours later. At first she didn't know where she was, for she had been dreaming of University Park. Then she heard a noise in the next room, and her lips turned up in a small, secret smile. The connecting door stood ajar. No need for barriers now. . . . She sat up, stretched, and pushed back her tangled curls. The candles were gone. But it had been no dream. Dreams left no traces on the skin, no such tracks across the heart. . . .

Nathan came into the room adjusting his cuff links. He was dressed for the office in a light-blue summer suit. Sitting down on the edge of the bed, he took up her hand and kissed the fingertips.

"Happy?" he asked.

"I've never been happier." She smoothed his lapels. "You're going to the office?"

"A budget meeting that may take all day. But I'll tell you what. We'll meet at the Trevi Fountain this afternoon. It's near my office. Then we can go on to the American Embassy and see about those wedding plans. You know about the Trevi?"

She shook her head.

"We'll throw in three coins. The first one assures that you'll return to Rome, the second that you'll find a husband, and the third that you'll be lucky in love. The second apparently doesn't ensure the third! And you have to do it just so—right hand over left shoulder."

"Are you superstitious?" Ashley teased. "I wouldn't have thought so."

"No," he winked, "but they work whether you believe in them or not." He checked his watch, then ogled her form under the sheet, which she held to her bosom. "Damn, the things a man has to forego in the name of schedules." He growled and kissed the tip of her nose. "Four-thirty at the fountain?"

After he had gone, Ashley bathed and dressed in a dreamy languor. Because her body still remembered him in spots, nearly every movement she made recalled an intimate moment. Often she paused at the mirror to marvel at the new, soft sensuality of her face and the unaccustomed fullness of her well-kissed lips. Everything had happened so fast, she reflected, in terms of the number of hours she had spent with him. But in another way it had taken a long time. For hadn't she been waiting her whole life for him, without knowing it? Mrs. Nathan Trent. It would take some getting used to, but in her bones she knew it was right. Already she felt herself changing subtly, preparing to assume the new layer of identity that marriage confers.

Humming to herself, she took out the Victorian-style, off-white dress she had worn to dinner at Nathan's house and sent it to be cleaned. He had asked her to be married in it, with her hair swept up as it had been that evening. Something old, something new—the dress, and the bone heels she had bought in Marseilles. Something borrowed? From someone at the embassy, perhaps. Anything would do. Something blue? She had to think. Then she recalled the sapphire birthstone ring among her jewelry. Yes, that would please Jean, her stepmother, who had given it to her for her fourteenth birthday. With the jewel case in her hand, Ashley paused to think of the woman who had always remained Jean and not Mama, who had always lived at a distance from her stepdaughter and even from her husband—not from a lack of love but from an inability to express that love. However, Jean would be glad for her now, and Ashley was eager to share her happiness. She went to the telephone.

"Ashley? Aren't you in Europe?" Jean's shy, surprised voice came at last from the modest ranch house in Arizona.

"In Rome." Ashley laughed. "How are you?"

"Fine. But—what's wrong? Why have you called? Has something happened?"

Ashley imagined her stepmother's anxious face. "Nothing's wrong. But something's happened, all right. I have good news and I just wanted to share it with you."

"With *me?*"

Ashley winced at the candor of Jean's disbelief. No, the gulf between them had not been all Jean's fault. That, Ashley was able to admit, was a measure of how much she had grown in the past few months.

Later, after a long and lively conversation, Ashley took a cab to the elegant shopping district around the Via Condotti, near where Nathan had bought her the blouse. Using money with which she had intended to pay her hotel bill, she bought a new perfume, some scandalously expensive lingerie, and a pair of handmade silver goblets, the last as a wedding present for Nathan and herself. Window-shopping and browsing, she eventually arrived in the neighborhood of the Pantheon, after the Colosseum perhaps the most famous monument in Rome. As she strolled in the cavernous interior with a number of others, a girl dressed in black, who appeared to be just another tourist, stepped to the center of the circular hall. Looking upward, toward the opening in the magnificent dome, through which the clouds could be seen, she began to sing. As the rich, solemn strains of *Ave Maria* filled the space, the sightseers one by one came to a halt. Swelling and doubling back on itself in echo, the voice filled the ancient structure as roundly as the pealing of a great bell. Ashley had the sensation of participating in a timeless celebration, older even than the Pantheon itself. At the end, the singer rejoined her group and slipped away, unknown and unapplauded. The listeners stirred, spoke, and soon the level of activity was back to normal. But no one who had been there, Ashley thought as she left, would ever forget the experience.

In a dusty print shop nearby, she found a nineteenth-century engraving of the very spot on the Palatine Hill where she and Nathan had sat and talked. This she bought for him as well. It made her happy to think of ways to make him happy, all the more so because he had told her about his tragic first marriage and she felt he'd already had his share of unhappiness.

By the time she returned to the hotel, she had just an hour to put away her purchases and freshen up before starting for the Trevi Fountain.

The clerk with whom she had spoken earlier was on duty. With her key, he handed her an envelope. "A message was left for you while you were out."

She knew, although she had never seen Nathan's handwriting, that the bold scrawl was his.

"Mr. Trent was here?" She fought back disappointment.

"No, Miss Sarti came for his things." The man moved over to attend to another guest, but not before Ashley fancied that she caught a gleam of amusement in his eye.

Unable to wait until she got to her room, she dropped her packages on the counter and tore open the envelope.

> Tried to reach you. Must fly to Marseilles overnight. Meet you at Trevi Fountain 4:30 tomorrow instead.
>
> N.

A chill crept over her. Of course he would be back. Was there any reason in the world to think otherwise? She read the note again. It was distant, impersonal.

"Excuse me, please." She broke into the clerk's conversation with the other guest. "Miss Sarti... is she Mr. Trent's secretary?"

"I couldn't say, Miss."

"Thank you." Hadn't Dominique made some insinuation about Nathan's secretary? Gathering up her bundles, Ashley fled for the elevator. Of course Nathan would be back. *I want to marry you...before anything can separate us again,* he had said. But she could not shake her premonition that something terrible was about to happen, or perhaps already had. When she got to her room, she found the connecting door had been locked. It had been the maid's doing, surely. Still, it seemed a bad omen.

By keeping busy, Ashley got herself in hand again. She bought American magazines and newspapers and read them. She did her nails. The hour when she was to have met Nathan passed. She finished her final story for the *Chronicle* and mailed it off. She wrote a letter of resignation to mail at the same time, but at the last moment kept it in her purse instead. For what if something *did* happen and Nathan did not return? Nevertheless, with a fine disregard for consistency, she cancelled her plane reservation. Burning her bridges one at a time instead of all at once, she twitted herself, as she stood at the window watching the sun go down. The room, formerly so tasteful and charming, now appeared dreary and empty, as if not even she herself were standing in it. Who was Miss Sarti? she wondered. On impulse, she decided to dress and go out.

To bolster her flagging spirits, she put on the blouse Nathan had bought her with her orchid suit and her favorite amethyst stud earrings. Splashing on her new perfume, she felt more cheerful. She didn't need company to enjoy herself! And besides, before she knew it Nathan would be back, to laugh with her at her misgivings.

Downstairs, she was pleased to see that a new clerk had come on duty. She gave him her name and room number.

"Are there any messages for me?"

The young man cast an eye back at the pigeonhole bearing her number. Looking past him, Ashley saw several message slips in Nathan's box.

"No, Miss Forrester. There are no messages."

"No phone calls? I was out briefly this afternoon." She was ashamed of the insecurity that showed in her voice.

"No, nothing. I'm sorry."

"Well, then," she said airily, mustering unconcern, "I'll be going out." But suppose he did phone? "No," she decided, "if there *should* be a call, I'll be in the hotel bar for a while."

"Very good, Miss."

At that hour the well-known bar was thronged with a varied, cosmopolitan crowd. Ashley took a small table along a wall, facing into the room. Ordering a Campari and orange juice, she settled back to amuse herself by trying to guess each person's country of origin, going on clothes and mannerisms. First off she recognized an English couple by the facial resemblance to her own relatives, for the Forresters were Anglo-Saxon through and through. Next she pegged a woman as French because of the distinctive way she had maximized the good points of her face and body without hiding her flaws. Only the French had that kind of security about fashion, she surmised. And then there was the whole range of Italian types to appreciate, from the dark-eyed, dark-haired people generally associated with the Mediterranean to blond, green-eyed men and women who looked as if they had stepped from the canvases of Botticelli.

It was, she realized suddenly, the first time she had ever been in a bar by herself. She had never even gone to a singles bar with her friends, although she had been asked often enough. Ashley leaned her chin on her palm and watched a waiter slide like a dancer through the crush, a tray of drinks balanced on one hand high above his head. This was enjoyable. The European bar seemed to be less of a refuge and more of an accepted meeting place than the American. For the third time she avoided the eyes of a man two tables away. About her own age, he had the smoothly deferential gaze of a professional woman pleaser. His sports coat was draped casually over his shoulders like a cloak, and his shirt was open halfway down his chest to display a heavy gold chain and medallion. He was slim and sleek and he reminded her of an otter. When she inadvertently met his eyes again, he gave her a sulky look from under his brows and flashed his teeth in a conspiratorial smile. Good Lord, she teased herself, did she look that desperate and lonely?

She turned her attention away but couldn't rid herself of the feeling that she was being scrutinized. It was a prickly sensation in her neck and shoulders, and it simply would not go away. A few minutes later, however, she saw her young man join another single woman at a table in the corner, and she had to laugh at herself. She still had a long way to go before the role of independent, traveling woman came easy to her. After she and Nathan were married, she reminded herself, she would have other chances to be on her own. The night before, they had spoken about the need for individual freedom as well as a shared life. Oh, if only Nathan were here right now, to share this evening. . . .

At that moment, with shocking abruptness, she learned why her feeling of being observed had persisted.

"Well, Tippy, how are you enjoying high society?" asked a voice behind her. Only one person in the world had ever called her Tippy. He'd given her the pet name himself.

Clayton Pridemore pulled out a chair and sat down.

chapter 10

"CLAYTON!"

"Not 'Clay' anymore?" He took the familiar cigarette case of chased silver from an inner coat pocket, extracted a cigarette, and tamped it on the edge of the table. He offered the case to her.

"You know I don't smoke," Ashley said.

"Correction. I know you didn't smoke. But when people travel, they sometimes feel free to do things they wouldn't do at home." He bent to light his cigarette and squinted shrewdly up at her through the smoke.

"Still master of the double meaning, I see," Ashley observed stonily. "Clay, what are you doing here?"

Clayton Pridemore summoned a waiter. With a glance at Ashley's drink, he ordered the same. "So you retain your fondness for Campari and orange juice. I hope you haven't forgotten who introduced you to it. Remember? The night we went to the Windjammer."

"I haven't forgotten." It hadn't been that long ago, she thought with a twinge. "But somehow I don't think you're here to discuss my drinking habits." She steeled herself against him. Once he had been able to talk her into anything.

"Ashley, Ashley. Relax. This is the land of *la dolce vita,* isn't it? There's no hurry." His drink arrived and he raised it to her. "To the future."

She let hers stay on the table. "You leave my future alone."

Clay smiled with satisfaction, sipping his drink and

letting his eyes wander over the crowd. Ashley watched him tensely. It was generally said that clothes make the man, but Clayton Pridemore made clothes look better than they were. He was sleek and smooth and—yes, something like that gigolo who had been staring at her, Ashley thought. With his perfectly styled hair and tinted glasses, he could have stepped from the pages of the latest men's fashion magazine. His look was unquestionably attractive, but it was totally manufactured. He had none of the rough edges, the untamed quality, that characterized Nathan's appearance, despite the latter's equal attention to detail.

Clay turned back to her. "How well I know you, Tippy. You're sitting there, shaking in your shoes, because I've shown up here. Because you look at me and feel that little tug of emotion that—"

"Why *have* you shown up?" she broke in. "You still haven't answered that."

He held up a calming hand. "We'll get to that. But first I want to say that the travel pieces you've sent have been first-rate. A couple of them I would even rank among your best work. Do you know, we've had several letters asking if you're going to be writing a regular column? I've been running them under the heading "Forrester's Europe" to give the series continuity."

"Thanks, I appreciate that," she allowed grudgingly. "How are things at the office?"

He stubbed out his cigarette. "Okay, on balance. Trudy is running herself ragged trying to do everything at once." Under the pretense of moving out of a waiter's path, he shifted his chair around so that he was beside her. "But you'll soon be back to take some of the burden off."

Ashley rubbed at a water spot on the table with her

forefinger. "I want to talk to you about that. I have a letter in my purse—"

"Oh, yes, the future. That's what the whole conversation is about, isn't it, Tippy? You know that and that's why you're afraid."

"The future?"

"Our future." He laid a hand on her arm.

"How *is* the new girl in advertising?" Ashley asked sharply and drew her arm away.

"Fine, I suppose," Clay responded coolly. "So Trudy has been keeping you informed."

"Not that I'm interested," Ashley hastened to say.

"Of course you are. After what we had? Baby, you couldn't be anything else."

Ashley met his gray eyes without a qualm. "What did we have, Clay? I'm not sure I can define it, because we each called it something different. I thought it was love, to be followed by engagement and marriage. That was too embarrassingly conventional for you. And to me, your 'open marriage' idea was just another name for an affair, with no more permanence to it than a snowflake."

To her surprise, he did not try to argue. "Yes, we were worlds apart then. But people change."

"Oh, really?"

"You have, my dear."

Caught off guard, she had to ask, "In what way?"

Clay studied her from behind the shaded barrier of his glasses. "For one thing, I suspect that your opinion on love affairs has broadened in recent weeks. Wouldn't you say so?"

A hot flash of color suffused her face. This was a reference to Nathan, she knew. "It's none of your business."

"Isn't it? You broke off with me. I didn't break off with you."

"Meaning?"

"Meaning that I still care for you. I just couldn't accept your terms."

"And you still can't," she argued.

"But you've relaxed your standards. We may not be as far apart as we were."

It was impossible to tell how serious he was, but she knew she could not afford to take his sudden appearance in Rome lightly. Swallowing her dislike of argument, she said, "Clay, this whole thing is ridiculous. Whatever we once had is broken beyond repair. I can't believe that you've come all the way to Rome to have another fight about it, but if you did, you've wasted a lot of time and money."

His arm found its way around her. "I've missed you, Tippy," he said in a manner that tried too hard to sound sincere. "After we broke off, we didn't talk privately for two or three months, remember? But you were there at the *Chronicle,* where I could see you now and then, and we never stopped discussing business." He shook his head in reminiscence. "It wasn't until you'd left for Europe that I realized how much that still mattered to me— to be able to see you often."

Could she believe any of it? Clay spoke with the overly careful diction of one who has risen too deliberately above his origins, and this always made him sound a little false. Once she would have given the world to hear him say such things. But now.... "I wouldn't give a plugged nickel for your motives, Clay."

"I don't blame you. I deserve it." He stopped the waiter and ordered a refill.

Ashley gave him a sidelong glance full of suspicion. Humility was not a Pridemore trait. Neither was accepting blame. "Tell me you came to Rome for some other reason. Tell me you're on vacation or on your way to a conference," she begged.

"Sorry." He flashed his patented, devil-may-care grin. "You're it, the one and only reason."

"But why?"

"I want you to come home with me."

"But . . . I would have come home soon anyway," she floundered.

"Would you?" He set fire to another cigarette.

Ashley watched the glittering figures moving in the mirror behind the bar. Of course. She was not the reason he had come, not precisely. Nathan was. Nathan was the unspoken subject of the conversation. She must not let herself forget that again.

"There's something you should know," she began, then paused to consider tactics. Better say it all at once and bear his taunts. "I said I had a letter in my purse. Well, it's a letter of resignation. I'm just coming home to close up my apartment and clear away things at the office. I'm not coming back to the *Chronicle*."

Something moved deep in his eyes, like a fish stirring in murky water. "Fine. You've anticipated me."

"How?"

"Sweetheart, in two months the *Chronicle* will have a new editor. I've handed in my resignation too."

Ashley sat back in astonishment. "I thought you liked your job. Where are you going?"

"Into television news. A big station in Los Angeles." He took a brochure from his breast pocket and laid it on the table. "I want you to come along. With your looks, poise and writing ability you could be a smash as a newscaster. Of course, you would have to have some training in oral presentation." He tapped the brochure. "Look at it. I have the power to hire you. We could close the deal tonight, on the spot."

"But television is such a different medium. You know how few make the transition successfully. I couldn't just—" She clapped her hands to her head. "Oh, what am I saying? I can't consider this. Clay, my whole life has changed since I left." She took a deep breath, then spilled it. "I'm going to marry Nathan Trent."

Clay began to laugh. "Marry you? He said that? The old boy's using big bait this time."

"It's no joke." Ashley glared at him. "As soon as he gets back from Marseilles, we're going to make arrangements at the American Embassy."

Clay pounced on this information with glee. "Oh, then he's already left you?"

"Stop it. I'm not going to let you cheapen this, Clayton Pridemore. Nathan and I . . . we . . . we love each other."

"Oh? And how do you know that?" He cocked an eyebrow.

"Well, he followed me to Rome. I turned him down in Marseilles but he didn't give up."

"Ah, the chase. Nathan always liked that part the best. But as for following you to Rome, I've come farther than he did," Clay reminded her.

"You don't understand. It's not just that. There's so much more that I can't explain." She sighed. She knew exactly what he was trying to do. He was attempting to undermine her confidence in Nathan so that he himself could step into the breach. Still, she could not completely discount his charges, for they matched her own earlier doubts. "He didn't push me into anything. We even have separate rooms."

"That only means that you've been upgraded from weekend fling to mistress."

"I said stop it!"

"I've got you going, haven't I?" Clay nodded. "You're

really not as sure of him as you pretend. Did I ever tell you about that poor English girl who spent her entire savings for a trousseau, on the strength of a few promises from Trent?"

"No, you didn't. And I don't want to hear it."

"I hope she found a use for all those monogrammed towels."

"It seems to me," Ashley said through a haze of fury, "that for you to criticize Nathan's marital intentions is for the pot to call the kettle black."

"Sure. We're two of a kind. I admit it." Clay polished his signet ring on his cuff. "If you don't trust me, why trust him?"

Ashley slumped in her chair. She had been tired before Clay showed up. Now she was exhausted. . . . He was wrong. He was lying. Feelings didn't lie. And she knew what Nathan and she felt. Clay had never felt like that about her, or she about him. She knew she had to keep on battling and not weaken. It was the only way to win. Win what? she wondered vaguely. She was even beginning to think like them.

"You're playing dog in the manger, is that it?" she asked tiredly. "You aren't interested in me. But you don't want me to have any happiness with Nathan either. Do you dislike me? Why can't we just go our separate ways?"

"Dislike you?" Clay took her hands across the table. "How long have we known each other?"

"Since I interned at the *Chronicle*. Three, no, four years ago. But of course it wasn't until—" She trailed off. Better not bring up old memories. Clay would find a way to turn them against her.

"It's been a long time, Tippy, and most of it good. Now you're willing to throw it all away for somebody you've known less than a month."

"But there's nothing to throw away!" Her voice rose hysterically. "How many times do I have to tell you? And the bottom line is it was wrong from the beginning!" She pulled her hands away and wrung them together in her agitation. "You never loved me. That was clear at the end. And I was in love with love."

Clay said nothing, but his eyes were wily as he surveyed their surroundings. The dinner hour was at hand. Where before had sat conservatively dressed businessmen and businesswomen, winding down from the day's work, now there were more formally attired groups bound for dinner or the nightclub scene.

"How deceptive appearances are," Ashley fretted. "They all look so happy. I wonder how many of them have another story to tell, as we do." And where was Nathan now? Was he alone? Her heart contracted with anguish. Clay's hints were having their effect.

And he knew it. He turned his attention back to her, exuding assurance. "You said you were resigning. What are your plans? After you marry, that is."

"Immediately? I don't know. We may travel."

"And then the proverbial rose-covered cottage?"

"I'd like to make a home for us," Ashley said awkwardly. "He doesn't have a real home."

Clay's shoulders shook with merriment. "You poor little child! Have you seen that palace in Marseilles? Do you expect to sew curtains for it?"

"At the risk of sounding trite, may I remind you that a house is not a home?" she snapped.

Clay patted her hand as one would soothe a pet. "Admit it, Tippy. You and Nathan haven't gotten around to discussing the future. And do you know why? Because His Majesty doesn't give a damn what happens to you after he's through with you."

"We did talk briefly about my continuing in journalism," Ashley offered desperately.

"Very briefly, I'm sure."

"Oh, for heaven's sake, be reasonable. We haven't had time to go into details. He was called away."

"Yes," Clay riposted, "Nathan would be moving too fast for details."

"How can you talk this way about him? He was your friend," she charged.

"You can't be friends with the rich unless you're rich yourself," Clay said shortly. "Don't you know that?"

"He isn't like that. He doesn't flaunt his wealth. Maybe I expected him to, but he hasn't."

"You can only be used by them," Clay persisted.

"He hasn't used me! I don't feel that I've been used."

"You will. Believe me, you will."

Ashley looked at him with curiosity. As well as she had known Clay, here was a dark side she had never seen. What had Nathan said? Clay could never forget that I was a Trent. . . .

After a time Clay said, "If you're smart, you'll come with me to L.A."

"Why?" Ashley asked.

"Isn't it obvious?"

"No, it isn't." She was impatient now, eager to be over and done with the conversation. "Are you only interested in me as a member of your news team? Am I really the best person for the job?"

"Of course."

"Or is the job just a bribe to get us back together?"

"Of course."

Ashley sighed explosively. "But why? Do you actually expect me to believe that you care for me?"

"Of course."

"Or do you merely want to come between Nathan and me?"

"Of course." From beneath half-closed lids, he watched her fume. Then he yawned elaborately. "It's all true. All of the above. You've stated the situation well, Tippy."

"Thank you."

"Yes," he nodded, "you've changed all right. You're tougher, less starry-eyed than you were six months ago. To be frank, I didn't expect you to put up such a fight here. I like it. How about going somewhere for dinner?"

But Ashley was not listening. "I suppose you found out from Trudy that I had changed my hotel," she said. "And you knew I couldn't afford to stay here on a reporter's salary." .

He nodded again.

Ashley regarded him sadly. To think that she had been willing to stake everything on this man, who hadn't the slightest inkling of what real affection was! And she might even have been content, because she hadn't known either. . . .

"Would you have come after me if I'd been alone? If I hadn't been with Nathan?" she inquired.

"Certainly." But from the way his eyes slid away from hers, she knew it wasn't true.

"You couldn't have known I would be alone tonight," she went on slowly. "So you were prepared to face him?"

"Why not?" Clay rapped. "I'm not afraid of him. However, I preferred to speak to you by yourself. I happened to know he would be in Marseilles this week."

A wave of uneasiness broke over her. "But how could you know? Something came up suddenly. He left me a note."

"Is that what he told you?" Clay was enjoying himself

again. "He went to an annual meeting of shareholders. It's held at the same time every year."

"No. He would have told me. He would have taken me with him."

"But he didn't," Clay pointed out. "You'd better check with the hotel management and see how many nights your room is paid for. You'll never see Nathan Trent again."

All this time Clay had been idly watching the comings and goings through the doorway to the lobby, with only an occasional glance at Ashley. Now, as she studied his smug expression from the side, she saw him flinch, as if he had been struck across the mouth.

She turned to see Nathan shouldering his way through the crowd, awesome in his anger.

"Hello, old man," Clay said shakily, rising to meet him. "When the cat's away, the mice will play."

chapter 11

NATHAN CAUGHT UP a chair from another table and slammed it down in front of them. Ignoring Clay's outstretched hand, he dropped his attaché case at his feet and sat down.

"I knew you would come! Didn't I tell you he would come back?" Ashley exclaimed, turning from one to the other. "Now we can straighten this out. Clay seems to think—" But a poisonous glare from Clay made her take another tack. "I . . . didn't expect you until tomorrow."

"Obviously."

Only then did she really look at his face. She could understand why he would be puzzled and even angry to see Clay, but not why he was regarding her with a coldness that amounted to loathing. "I was just sitting here all by myself and in walked Clay. Imagine that!" she said, hating the false vitality in her voice and feeling like a child who has been caught at the cookie jar.

Nathan didn't even bother to respond. His eyes, like lasers, shifted to his old friend. "So. It's been a long time."

"Yes, it has." Clay ran a finger under his collar.

"I hear you're leaving the *Chronicle*." Nathan waved the waiter away. "I'll be losing a good man."

"I never intended to stay forever."

"I never expected you to."

With unsteady hands Clay lit another cigarette. Afraid

to look at Nathan again, Ashley watched the operation as if her life depended on the outcome.

"It's a big step up," Clay resumed, exhaling smoke. "I'll have name recognition. More power. And—" His eyes narrowed and he nodded to himself.

"And?" Nathan prodded him.

"And I won't be a lackey of Trent Enterprises."

"Nobody made you take that job," Nathan said quietly. "And I didn't give it to you. You earned it. You were paid well. And given free rein." A vein beat in his temple. His civility to Clay was costing him dearly.

"That didn't make it any easier."

So, mused Ashley, the battle lines were drawn.

"Is that why you're here? To settle an old grudge?" Nathan asked.

"No, no." Clay flipped a hand. "I came to see Ashley."

She wanted to reach out and touch Nathan, physically to turn aside, somehow, the course of the conversation. But it was too late. Maybe it had been too late from the day they'd met.

"That's the same thing, isn't it?" Nathan snapped. "Isn't she just a pawn in this?"

"Now wait a minute," Ashley protested. "I don't like being discussed as if I weren't even here."

"Better be quiet and listen, love," Clay advised her. "You might learn something you need to know. This is going to get interesting."

She shrank back, wounded. Just a pawn in their game. And it was Nathan who had admitted it, not Clay. All the fight went out of her.

Nathan unbuttoned the remaining button of his suit jacket and loosened his tie. He shot his cuffs and folded his hands before him on the table. "I was suspicious from the beginning," he said to Clay. "Sorry to disappoint you on that score."

Clay flicked ashes into the ashtray. "Oh, how's that?"

"She was so poorly prepared. She picked me up in a restaurant in Marseilles and tried to get an interview out of me," Nathan drawled. "It was an inept job if I ever saw one, yet she seemed to be fairly intelligent. So I knew right away that it wasn't her idea, that someone had put her up to it. And of course as soon as she mentioned the *Chronicle*—" He spread his hands wide and shrugged. "You should have coached her better."

"But that was the beauty of it," Clay said with a certain relish. His jitters were gone. "If I'd coached her, she wouldn't have been as appealing. Ashley is so wonderfully vulnerable, don't you think? It's one of her greatest charms."

"Yes, I suppose you're right," Nathan nodded, businesslike.

"Besides, if I'd explained that it was to be a joke on you, she wouldn't have gone along with it. Ashley"—and here his voice became snide—"is a lady of principles. Or so she has always led me to believe."

"Then she's an innocent in this?" Nathan asked carefully.

Clay paused to consider the point, giving Ashley time to reflect that they were like boxers circling each other, each one trying to anticipate the strategy of the other, each one jabbing away while he looked for a chance to throw the knockout punch.

"That depends on your definition of innocence," Clay said finally. "She didn't share my motives, but I think she quickly developed motives of her own for pursuing you."

It hit home. Nathan swallowed and cleared his throat.

But he was in control again when he proposed, "Explain her motives to me, Clayton. Maybe I haven't figured them all out yet."

"Glad to oblige." Clay held up an index finger. "First of all, there's the usual one of money. As a student at Creighton, and later as a reporter for the *Chronicle,* she would have heard all the lore and legend of the Trent fortune. Every coed at Creighton dreams of meeting a Trent, doesn't she? I gave Ashley the opportunity of a lifetime by suggesting she interview you."

"That's not true!" Ashley blazed. "I told you I didn't care anything about your money, Nathan. I only cared about—" she choked with emotion "—you."

"Well, now, that was very clever of you to bring the subject of money out in the open," Clay observed. "That way he couldn't accuse you later of hiding anything."

Speechless with frustration, Ashley bowed her head.

"Tell me some more about her motives," Nathan pressed. "You seem to know Ashley remarkably well."

"I know her a good deal better than you do, old man," Clay said cockily. "And I know you even better than I know her. Motive number two—she wanted to get back at me."

"Why would she want to do that?" Nathan was sardonic. "You'll have to explain everything to me, remember. I'm the outsider in this, I now realize."

He was laughing at all of them, including himself, Ashley thought miserably. He was enjoying the confrontation.

"We-ell, I'm too much of a gentleman to go into details," Clay went on, pulling a righteous face. "But as you must know, Ashley and I nearly got married last year. I think she still harbors some bad feelings about the breakup. She blames me."

"Do you?" Nathan asked her.

Ashley took her time before saying levelly, "I'm not going to answer that or any other question. I'm not going to be a party to this. Neither one of you has any right to interrogate me." But behind her brave front she was dying by inches. Nathan was going over to Clay's side. She could sense him turning against her. In their eagerness to hurt each other, the two did not notice or did not care that she was trapped in the middle, catching all the blows.

Clay rattled change in his pocket. "She knew what she was doing when she went after you. She knew you and I had our differences and that it would be a slap in my face if she snared you."

"And was it?" Nathan demanded.

"No," Clay answered, but Ashley noticed that he had begun to perspire lightly. "Snare and snare alike, I say, just like always."

"Yes, just like in the good old days," Nathan agreed, a wry twist to his lips. "But if Ashley's motive was revenge, she had to let you know about her 'success' with me. Did she write to you?"

"She didn't have to. It was all in the stories for the *Chronicle,* although you were never mentioned by name. The description of the dinner party in Marseilles gave it away. And even the latest one, with her observations on the Roman ruins. It too had the Trent flair. She was seeing Europe through your eyes. I knew she was with you." And here, at last, his voice betrayed him. It was thick with bitterness, and in spite of herself, Ashley felt sorry for him.

"I didn't do it to hurt you," she broke in. "That never entered my mind. I swear to you, Clay, that what has happened—" For an instant she paused, embarrassed, before finishing, "What has happened has nothing to do with you."

"Clay doesn't want to believe that," Nathan remarked. "Because if you didn't want to hurt him, then maybe the only explanation is that you and I fell in love."

All at once it was very quiet. Ashley noticed that the room was empty save for the bartender and two customers standing at the bar. In another part of the hotel, an orchestra was playing *Siboney*. She looked beseechingly at Nathan, searching for a spark of emotion that would back up what he had just said. *Yes,* she begged silently, *admit that we fell in love.* But his face was as still and as devoid of feeling as that of a statue.

"Love!" Clay rasped. "Then let me tell you about her chief motive. She's ambitious, is our Ashley. If she got an interview with you, she wouldn't waste it on the *Chronicle*. Oh, no. She'd sell it to a national magazine and open all kinds of doors for herself."

"And that's the reason you haven't received the interview from her? She's saving it to peddle for big money?"

"Or she's still collecting information," Clay speculated. "Maybe if you hang around long enough you can write a whole book, Tippy. *My Life with Nathan Trent: A Personal Memoir.* Every drugstore in America would want to stock it."

The waiter appeared to ask after their comfort and went away again. Ashley had seen Nathan grimace at Clay's use of her nickname. Perhaps he wasn't as uninvolved as he appeared. In fact, she was beginning to realize that Nathan had controlled the conversation from the start—and not Clay, as she had thought. Clay was doing most of the talking, but Nathan was asking the questions. She sat up straighter. He was interviewing

Clay, as he had interviewed her at their first meeting. He was turning Clay inside out and Clay didn't even know it. Clay thought he was winning, but he didn't even see what Nathan's strategy was. Did she see? she wondered. What was the point in leading Clay on, in hearing all of the damaging things he had to say, especially about her? Was he just checking Clay's story against hers, and vice versa, like a good journalist?

A jolt of pure panic shot through her. What if he were using Clay as his mouthpiece, letting Clay lay out all the reasons why Nathan shouldn't marry her? Was Clay right about Nathan? Was this a grotesque good-bye? No, that was crazy. Nathan must know that Clay was lying. He had to! But she couldn't be certain. At one time or another, early in their acquaintance, Nathan had suspected her of every one of those motives himself.

While she had been pondering the situation, the two men had wandered off on a minor point about something that had happened to them in Cleveland. Now Nathan swung back to the matter at hand.

"You've done an excellent job in explaining Ashley to me, Clay," he said, with the faint note of disgust he had maintained throughout the exchange. "I wouldn't have thought her to be so conniving, but there you are. You've known her far longer than I have. Now what about me? Would you care to venture a theory about why I've shown so much interest in her, a small-town reporter of no particular background or accomplishment?"

"Hey." Clay frowned his reproof. "Ashley doesn't want to hear this."

Her eyes were moist, but for once she didn't care whether she cried or not. "Go on," she told Clay. "At this point you can't possibly surprise me. Or embarrass me further."

"Okay, but what can I say?" Clay asked Nathan. "For the same reason you went after all the others. For the good times. We're two of a kind, you and I."

"You forget I gave that up once, when I married."

"But who knows how that would have turned out?" Clay argued. "The accident was an awful tragedy, of course. No question about it. But at least there was no chance to become disillusioned."

"You monster," Ashley breathed.

A dull flush crept up Nathan's neck. His hands clenched into fists, and it seemed impossible that he could restrain himself from smashing Clay in the face. Slowly, however, his boiling rage subsided into a cold, crystalline state that could only be hatred. "There's just one person unaccounted for now," he said, "and that is you, Pridemore. What's your game? You said you came to see Ashley. To save her from throwing herself away on a rotter like me, no doubt?" His eyes crackled with contempt.

"Not exactly. I've offered her a job working for me in L.A."

Nathan looked sharply at her, his question evident.

"No, of course not," Ashley stammered. "You know I wouldn't consider it. I have a commitment to you." She caught her breath. "Or . . . don't I?"

"Do you?"

"Be honest with him, Tippy," Clay interrupted them. "You *were* tempted by my offer. Right away you started to worry about shifting from one news medium to another. Don't let that vulnerability fool you, my man." He winked at Nathan. "She's that new breed of loner, the dedicated career woman."

"So she told me in Marseilles."

"But I was only speaking in general about the problems of the job. I wasn't talking about taking it. You know that, Clay. You're twisting my words." She pressed her lips together to keep them from trembling.

"Just a business deal? Is that all you're offering?" Nathan taunted his rival. "It's not like you to miss the personal angle."

"I'm not. If she comes with me, we pick up where we left off. Don't we, Tippy? And besides, I guarantee you that your name will be a household word in California in five years."

"'Baby, I'm gonna make you a star,'" Nathan jeered.

"Then top it. Make her a better deal."

Nathan glanced at his watch and straightened his tie, as if he were about to leave. The lines of anger in his face smoothed out. He had come to a decision. "No offer. Sorry."

"What's this? Are the stakes too high, old man? Didn't you tell me once that your great-great-grandfather bet his wife against a keg of whiskey, out on the frontier?" Clay goaded him.

"Yep. But maybe I don't play the game the way my great-great-grandfather did." Nathan's smile was tinged with melancholy, and his thoughts appeared to be elsewhere. For a moment his eyes rested on Ashley almost quizzically, as if he were trying to remember where he had seen her before.

The sudden collapse of Nathan's position startled Ashley. Just when she most wanted him to take charge and call Clay's bluff, he was folding. Why? She almost would have preferred a real fight, as between the boxers she had imagined them to be, instead of this war of words. Too much could be hidden by words.

"No proposal of marriage after all?" Clay threw an I-told-you-so look Ashley's way.

"No. You can deal me out." Nathan continued to fix his attention on Clay, ignoring Ashley. "You might say

I've decided that the game isn't worth the candle after all."

Briefly Ashley closed her eyes, while the pain sank in.

Clay took out two airplane tickets and laid them on the table exactly as if he were displaying a winning poker hand. "All right, Tippy, you heard what the man said. Now what shall it be?" When she didn't answer, he added with a touch of impatience, "What do you say?"

Slowly she raised her head to consider each of them in turn. "What do I say? I'm surprised you thought to ask. Does the turkey in a Thanksgiving raffle have any say about who wins it? You don't care what I think."

"But I do," Clay insisted. "Nathan has made his decision alone. I'm letting you decide about us."

"No," Ashley told him. "It doesn't matter what I say. And it doesn't matter to you whether I go with you or not. Because you've won, Clayton. You've forced your adversary out of the contest. That's all you really wanted. I was just a means to that end. The pawn, remember?"

Clay started to protest but he stopped when Ashley rose to her feet. She looked down at Nathan. "And I guess you got what you wanted too, and a little more. A little more than that single day of my time you asked for in Marseilles." A single tear fell from her cheek onto the silk rose at her breast, staining a petal. "Are you satisfied?" she asked softly.

Pain appeared to flicker in his eyes but she told herself it was only acute embarrassment. "Ashley, I—" He ran a hand through his hair. For once in his life, Nathan Trent was at a loss for words.

Ashley shouldered her bag and walked away. She never looked back. Behind her, dead silence reigned.

chapter 12

IN HER HASTE, Ashley forgot to press the elevator button for her floor and was carried to the top of the hotel. When the doors opened, she found herself looking out on a sun-bathing area adjacent to a kidney-shaped swimming pool. She stepped out and the elevator went away. Someone had left a champagne glass on an iron patio table nearby. The entire roof was deserted. A lone deck chair stood at the water's edge. It seemed to beckon her, promising peace and quiet.

Ashley sat down, curling her legs under her, and stared into the pool, which underwater lights turned a glowing turquoise. The night breeze sent occasional shivers of silver over the surface. After the close atmosphere of the bar, the fresh air felt wonderful on her flushed cheeks. Far below, the streets of Rome purred in their sleep. She wondered if Nathan and Clay were still talking downstairs, or if they had come to blows.

Later, she knew, she would be sad and hurt. Now she was angry. She and Nathan had that in common, she reflected. They were both quick to anger and quick to calm down again. Clay was another matter. He had the dangerous habit of holding grudges, as he had so amply demonstrated that evening. She drummed her fingers on the chair arm until she made herself jumpy. The injustice of it all rankled deeply. They had pawed over her character as if it were a piece of sale merchandise. Neither one of them had given her a chance to defend herself. Or rather, Clay had done the pawing. But Nathan had not prevented him. Clay's asking her to make the final decision was only a piece of bravado. He had hoped she would choose him over Nathan in Nathan's presence, so that his triumph would be complete. How wrong he had been, she thought, and got up to walk.

The sound of a car horn floated up from the distant street, and she strolled over to the surrounding parapet surmounted by grillwork and looked down. A taxi was pulling away from the main entrance. Could it be Clay leaving? She decided it was, since it was getting late and little other traffic was moving on the street. That would mean Nathan was on his way to his room. All at once the logjam of confusion in her mind broke, and her future was clear to her.

She would take a two-month leave of absence from the *Chronicle*. During that time, she might accept Jean's invitation to visit in Arizona. More important, she would look aggressively for another job. First off, she would inquire at *Land and Sea,* a travel monthly based in Tampa, which was about to undergo a reorganization of its staff. If nothing came through, then she could go back to the *Chronicle* after Clay had left. But not to stay. She was beginning to see why someone might want to leave Trent Enterprises. Even from a distance, Nathan's power and magnetism would sap her own strength. She would not be able to think clearly or to feel in control of her destiny as long as his presence imposed itself on her through the *Chronicle*.

Fired with new determination, Ashley started for the stairs. She couldn't even wait for the elevator, because first, before she went ahead with her future, she had a score to settle.

Tripping down the stairs, she rehearsed what she was going to say. Nathan had made fun of her journalistic skills in Marseilles, but in his just-finished discussion with Clay, he had broken every rule in the book, and she intended to tell him so. He had accepted Clay's conjectures in place of facts. That meant he had taken slander for the truth. He had not asked to hear her side, although she knew the facts better than anyone. That was like neglecting to question the chief witness to a murder—or in this case, to a character assassination, she thought with annoyance. Worst of all, he had let his personal feelings interfere with his "investigation" of her. If any employee of his did the same on assignment, he would be fired.

Her footsteps slowed as she came to Nathan's door, but she passed on to her own room. Despite her high-flying resolve, she needed a moment more to compose herself before facing His Majesty for the last time.

The first thing she saw when she opened the door was her intended wedding dress, back from the cleaners and hanging against the wall in a plastic wrapper. Anguish twisted through her. It would never be used for that now. Even if she convinced Nathan of the absurdity of Clay's allegations, there was still the fact that Nathan had withdrawn his marriage proposal. Impetuously she shut the dress out of sight in an armoire. As she did so, she heard a noise from the next room and assumed that Nathan had returned.

Although she knew it didn't matter how she looked for such a confrontation, still Ashley could not keep from checking her face in the mirror. Her eyes were abnormally large and bright. Perhaps it was excitement, or perhaps fear. She pinned up a loose strand of hair, ran a powder puff under her eyes and across her nose, and took her key to the connecting door out of a drawer. She was counting on her reporter's ability to deal with anyone, any time, to carry her through the next few minutes. That, she reminded herself sternly, and the responsible journalist's concern for truth.

Early in her career, when she had tried a little of everything to gain experience, Ashley had witnessed fires, arrests, and accidents with fellow reporters who covered such events. On those occasions she had often been struck by the way irrelevant details stand out against the background of tragedy—the rag doll that miraculously survives a fire and lies soaked and smudged in the smoldering ruins of a house; the half-done sweater, with knitting needles still stuck in, that is thrown clear in a car crash. Now, as she pushed open the door to Nathan's room, she had reason to recall that phenomenon. Her eye fell first on a two- or three-inch rip in a seam. Next she noticed that the seam was in the bodice of a ruffled orange taffeta dress thrown across a chair near the door. Only after observing these details did she realize that the dress belonged to Dominique, who stood before the dresser mirror in black patent dancing pumps, black fishnet stockings, and a black satin teddy, combing her wavy red hair.

Catching a glimpse of Ashley in the glass, Dominique put down the comb with impertinent slowness, propped her elbow on the dresser, and swung around, lounging against the piece of furniture much as she had leaned against the piano in her restaurant act.

"It's Ashley, isn't it?" she inquired in her richly accented, honey-smooth voice. She was anything but ill at ease.

"Yes, that's right." Ashley's practiced eye catalogued the flawless skin, the heart-shaped beauty spot on the cheek, the generously endowed and well-proportioned figure, which showed up her own as too slender and straight. From the orange dress, dancing shoes, and the black ribbon around Dominique's neck, it was obvious that she had just come from one of her shows and that she was supposed to resemble a can-can girl. Because of the fineness of the costume and Dominique's poise and beauty, the effect was dramatic and not at all tawdry, as it might have been on a less majestic woman.

"Come in, then." Dominique yawned. "Is Nathan expecting you?"

Ashley took one reluctant step across the threshold. All she could think was, So Clay had been right after all. "I don't exactly know how to answer that."

"Then he isn't." Dominique winked broadly. "I'll tell you a little secret. He's not expecting me either. Not exactly."

"Not exactly?" Ashled echoed.

"I would never tell him ahead of time. I prefer to be spontaneous," Dominique explained, crossing to the bed and sitting down on the edge. The covers had been turned back. "I came straight here from my last show. It's more exciting this way, don't you think?"

"I wouldn't know." She also didn't know what to do next. She shifted from one foot to the other, wondering how to manage a dignified exit.

"So you're staying in the next room," Dominique remarked, spreading out the fingers of one hand to study her nails. "How serious is it between you?"

"I'd rather not discuss it. It's a private matter."

"Then it's not as serious as you would like it to be," Dominique concluded. "Why do you need separate rooms, after all?"

"I think I should be going," Ashley stated flatly.

"What's your hurry?" Dominique smiled lazily. "I don't have anything to do until Nathan comes and who knows where he is?"

"He's downstairs. I left him just a few minutes ago.

I imagine he'll be here soon."

Dominique went to Nathan's armoire and began to search among the clothing hanging there. The clothing, at least, proved that he had intended to come back all along, Ashley mused. But knowing that only perplexed her more. Meanwhile, Dominique found Nathan's terrycloth robe and slipped it on.

"I'm not crazy, you know," she explained over her shoulder. "I looked here for a woman's clothes when I first came in. When I didn't find any, I thought he was alone. So I'm as surprised to see you as you are to see me." She gave an artful laugh, almost singing it, and plumped herself down in Nathan's desk chair, leaving the robe open. "Ooh, I'm tired. I think I'll have some champagne sent up."

"You seem quite at home. Do you come here often?" Catty, but Ashley didn't care.

"Oh, no." Dominique was almost insulted. "Nathan has only been a pleasant memory to me for many years. But I'm sure he'll be glad to see me. And from the way you're acting, I don't think I'm breaking up anything very important."

"Then you don't intend to leave?" Ashley asked.

"One of us will have to." The singer was friendly but unbending.

"But you're married to Alfredo, who owns the restaurant," Ashley blurted out in frustration.

Dominque shook her head. "Did Nathan tell you that? A lot has happened since his last visit to Rome."

"Isn't divorce impossible in Italy?" Ashley was recalling the problems of a famous film star that had been much in the news.

"I'm not an Italian citizen," Dominique told her, "so that's not my problem."

"But you were singing in Alfredo's restaurant just the

other night," Ashley pointed out.

"Why not? His regular singer was ill and I didn't mind helping out. Alfredo and I can still be friends." She patted her hair in a way that reminded Ashley of a preening pouter pigeon. "What else did Nathan tell you about me?"

"Just that you went to Greece together once," Ashley allowed grudgingly.

"Nathan is such a gentleman." Dominique sighed reminiscently. "It was a wonderful holiday—Athens, Rhodes, and a tiny island owned by one of his friends. I've never had such a tan! And the food. And the scenery. And the nights. And how long ago it was. . . ." She came abruptly back to the present. "Have you known him long?"

"Not long."

"It must be boring for you alone here all day," Dominique observed, as if she had all the time in the world to chat. "Nathan is such a, how do you say it, a slave driver. He's always at the office."

"I have my own work to do," Ashley said with asperity. "I'm not being 'kept,' if that's what you're thinking."

"Do you work for him? Surely you haven't replaced Miss Sarti." Dominique straightened her leg from the knee and turned her ankle this way and that, admiring her calf.

"No."

"Really, it's silly of me to think that anyone *could* replace Fabiana Sarti," Dominique prattled on. "Have you met her?"

"No. But I've heard of her." The conversation with Dominique had so far been merely irritating. But at the mention of Miss Sarti, Ashley's interest, against her will, soared. "What's she like?"

"Indescribable." The other woman shrugged. "I once

told Nathan that Miss Sarti is the only woman he really cares about. The rest of us mean nothing to him. I even said he should marry her and be done with it!" She laughed uproariously, but Ashley did not see the joke.

"Is she his secretary?"

"Oh, she's much more than a secretary. She's absolutely indispensable to him." Dominique leaned forward, enjoying the chance, even in such an unusual situation, to gossip. "She spoils him and he lets her. They're quite devoted to each other, in a way. I believe she's the only woman in the world who has influence over him."

Had the monogrammed cuff links been one of Miss Sarti's gifts to him? "Doesn't that bother you, Dominique, competing with the formidable Miss Sarti?" Ashley asked.

"Oh, I'm not competing with anyone," Dominique declared, and then added slyly, "unless you and I are competing now."

"Not me," Ashley stated with complete frankness. "I know when I'm out of my league. The way all of you trade back and forth and still remain friends—you and Nathan and Clay and Miss Sarti and Alfredo. It's a life I know nothing about."

"Miss Sarti?" Dominique looked confused. "I think you must have been given the wrong idea. But who is Clay?"

"Don't you know him?"

"No," said Dominique. "Should I?"

"Probably. Yes, you two would probably get along famously," Ashley said dryly. "Maybe Nathan could introduce you." She took the door key out of her pocket and crossed to where Dominique was sitting. "See that Nathan gets this, will you, please? It will keep people like me from walking in on him—and his friends—unexpectedly."

Dominique's large brown eyes sparkled. "You're going?"

"Yes, I leave the field to you. I only wanted to talk to him and now it's hardly necessary. So, good-bye. Knowing you has been very enlightening," Ashley finished, with a heavy irony that Dominique did not miss.

Dominique stood and gathered Nathan's robe around her comfortably. "It's too bad, isn't it?" she remarked. "After one gets to be a certain age, every man she meets had too much of a past." Pleasantly patronizing, she ended, "You're a sweet girl. You should have settled down with a husband long ago to have lots of pretty blond children."

Back in her room, Ashley took out her luggage and began to pack. She felt calm and clearheaded but drained, as she used to feel after final exams. She hesitated over the presents she had bought for Nathan. Although she didn't want the silver goblets, she wasn't generous enough to leave them for him to toast Dominique or another. She rolled them up in her nightgowns and put them in her smaller suitcase. They would make a nice wedding present for one of her friends someday.

Under a lamp she examined the engraving of the Palatine Hill. By her own standards she had spent a great deal of money for it, although the sum would be nothing for a man of Nathan's means. It was a good piece of work, too, and would not be out of place in Nathan's art collection. As she had no desire to keep it as a remembrance, she propped the engraving against the dresser mirror so that he would know she meant to leave it behind. He could consider it as her share of the hotel bill.

Strangely, she did not feel bitter toward him, but rather more disappointed with herself for having been taken in. She had expected the leopard to change his spots for her, and now she was paying for such unrealistic expectations. Looking at the engraving one last time, it was hard for her to believe that they had ever sat in that scene and talked, that they had ever shared an intimate moment. The idea was as remote as the civilization of ancient Rome.

As she walked down the hall to the elevator, she faintly heard Dominique singing.

chapter 13

WALKING INTO THE LOBBY, Ashley saw them before they saw her. They were standing in front of the glass double doors leading to the street, talking. So Clay hadn't left after all. Immediately she was struck by the change in each of them. Clay had lost his brash overconfidence and looked merely tired. He was speaking in a low voice to Nathan, gesturing fitfully with yet another cigarette. From the beginning, the chain-smoking had been an index of his uneasiness, Ashley remarked to herself. Nathan, on the contrary, stood comfortably wtih his hands in his pockets, nodding at something Clay was saying and smiling a little. To Ashley's exasperation, he looked like a man without a care in the world.

After asking the night clerk to call her a taxi, she continued to observe them for a few moments without making her presence known. Although each looked the part of the successful business executive, their styles contrasted. Clay was groomed and dressed to such perfection that he actually lacked individuality, while Nathan, with his tumbled hair, broken nose and ranginess, looked as if he had more important things on his mind than conforming to an image. He gave the impression, as always, of being utterly indifferent to what others thought of him, yet at the same time sent the clear message that he thought a great deal of himself.

Had the two at long last settled their differences? Ashley wondered as she walked toward them with her suitcases. They looked friendly enough.

At the sight of her, Clay took a step backward in surprise. He looked pointedly at her luggage and then to Nathan for an explanation.

Nathan looked her up and down, his face giving nothing away. "Where are you going?" he asked conversationally.

She hadn't thought that far ahead. On the spur of the moment, she remembered something she had read the day before. "To the railroad station. I think there's a service there that finds rooms for tourists."

"Not at this hour."

Ashley lifted her chin and met his eyes square on. It was false bravado, but he didn't have to know that. "Then I'll find a room some other way. It doesn't matter."

"You're welcome to stay upstairs," he drawled. "You can lock yourself in if you feel you have to. Any reason why you can't do that?"

"Yes. The reason is up in your room wearing black lingerie," Ashley informed him levelly. But something was wrong, terribly wrong. The feeling of triumph, of being in the right, that she had expected, did not come. And the look of complete puzzlement on Nathan's face was not the reaction she would have expected from the heartless rake she now believed him to be.

"Who?" he demanded.

"You mean which one of the many possibilities?" Ashley dared to say. "It's . . . Dominique."

"Dominique?" He swore under his breath.

Nathan's bafflement was real, Ashley thought distractedly, but it was too late for explanations. Too much had happened. She had the sensation of being on a runaway roller coaster that could not be stopped or turned back. Just then a pair of headlights shone in their direction.

"I think that must be my taxi now," she said, her voice not quite as steady as it had been before.

Clay had been watching them with an open-faced wonder peculiar in an adult. To Ashley, he looked like a small boy gawking at major league ballplayers. Unexpectedly he declared, "No, it's mine. I've been waiting longer than you have."

She frowned at him quizzically. Why would Clay want to leave her alone with Nathan? She didn't want that! "In that case, may I share it with you?" she proposed. "I'd like to leave now."

Clearly at a loss, Clay again looked to Nathan for a cue.

Trent shrugged. "Whatever the lady wants." He rocked back on his heels, the picture of unconcern.

"Let's go, Clay," Ashley said quickly. Both men made a move for her luggage. "Thank you, but I can carry them myself," she interposed in a small but determined voice. She kept her eyes down.

Clay went on ahead to say something to the driver. Noting that he had no suitcase with him, Ashley wondered how long he had been in Rome. A doorman appeared, but Nathan had already stepped forward to hold the door for her. Out of the corner of her eye, she saw that he was standing straight and tall and solemn faced. Making fun of her attempts at dignity, she decided.

She intended to pass him with her head down and without speaking, but circumstances dictated otherwise. Somehow her suitcases, shoulder bag, and portable typewriter all got tangled with her legs and she stumbled. The luggage scattered in all directions and Nathan caught her.

With his hands under her arms, he raised her slowly until she was on her feet again, but he did not release her. Spreading his fingers on her back, he exerted just enough pressure so that she would have to struggle to get away.

"Look at me," he ordered.

As she sank into the depths of his eyes, where lambent, blue flames of passion played, she forgot the present—Clay, the taxicab, her promises to herself, Dominique. Time had stopped. She was in his arms again.

"Do you really think you can walk away from this?" he asked seriously. "Do you really think you can forget?"

She remembered his lips on hers, and his cheek nuzzling her shoulder, and his heart pounding under her palm the way hers was pounding now. She remembered holding hands in the carriage and the smell of burning candles, and his face in candlelight, and the way he stood like a king among the guests in his own house. She would never forget any of those things, or the way his glasses slid down his nose, or the heartiness of his laugh, or the hollow at the small of his back. And the way their thoughts meshed when they talked, so that sometimes they tripped over each other's speech. She would look a long time before she found that again. And above all else, there would remain the simple, unalterable fact that she had loved him and had felt her love returned. . . .

She closed her eyes and leaned her forehead against his chest. With an effort, she dredged up the dark side of memory—Renata, Dominique, Miss Sarti. Nathan's original, frank intentions of seducing her. The abandoned marriage proposal. Tempted beyond reason to stay where she was, sheltered from reality in the circle of his arms, she was shaken by a long, shuddering sigh. But when she raised her eyes again to his, she had found the strength to stammer out, "No, I can't forget. I will carry you with me for the rest of my life. But I'm going, Nathan. Surely, knowing me as you do, you can understand why."

"Yes, I can. And you've told me all I want to know." The lines in his face crinkled with affection. "Good-bye, my love." Before Ashley could gather her wits about her, he had kissed her and let her go.

She stood in a daze, barely aware that the cabdriver was collecting her baggage and stowing it in the trunk. "I don't understand *you,* Nathan Trent. It's been like— like dancing in the dark with a man in a mask." She fled down the steps.

Clay, who had been waiting beside the taxi, helped her in and shut the door. He exchanged a few words with Nathan, who had come forward for that purpose, then walked around to the other side and got in.

As they pulled away, Nathan raised a hand in brief salute. He then turned and ambled back to the hotel with a lordly nonchalance.

Ashley drew her skirt down over her knees and otherwise arranged herself for the ride, but her thoughts were still back at the hotel, with the man who had let her go away with his old rival without regret, anger, or apology. It was almost as if he expected to see her again, she brooded, though how could that be? She was going back to the States on the first available flight, and it was highly unlikely that the paths of the publishing magnate and the small-town reporter would ever cross again. Besides, she reminded herself bitterly, she did not want to see him. His path was at that moment crossing Dominique's.

Sadly she watched the black buildings stream by. Never to see Nathan again—it was like being told that

she would never again see snowdrifts or autumn leaves
or spring flowers. It was like knowing that summer had
come for the last time.

"Aren't you listening?" Clay asked. "I said, the driver
wants to know where to go. Do you have any idea what
your plans are?"

His manner was carefully impersonal. He was sitting
as far away from her as possible. Once more Ashley
wondered what had passed between him and Nathan in
her absence.

"I'm sorry. I don't know," she admitted sheepishly.
"I'm too upset to think. Do you have any suggestions?"

"I'm staying with friends. So I can't offer—"

"No," she said swiftly. "I wasn't going to ask you
to."

"Don't worry," Clay rejoined with a touch of venom,
"I wasn't going to suggest we spend the night together."

"Maybe I should just go to the railroad station or the
airport. It's probably too late to get a room," Ashley
said, hoping Clay wouldn't start on their relationship
again.

"Nothing doing. He told me to see that you found a
decent place to stay."

"Nathan did? And you're willing to do it?" Ashley
was amazed.

"Yes." Clay was curt, faintly embarrassed.

"And he trusted you to do it?"

"I think," Clay observed in a pettish tone that dis-
couraged further probing, "he trusted you."

"But why would he even care?" Ashley almost wailed.
Although it hurt to do so, she made herself confess, "You
were right about him after all. I guess you knew him
better than I did."

And again she was surprised, for Clay was not particularly pleased to hear it. "People do change, as we said earlier," he remarked shortly. After a brief silence, he changed the subject. "I'll ask the driver about hotels."

"I'm sorry to put you to the trouble. Really I am. I should have waited for my cab."

"No apology necessary." He sat forward and began to query the driver, who understood some English.

Gladly Ashley let him take charge. Weary and disoriented, she decided that independence wasn't what it was cracked up to be. Everybody needed to be taken care of some of the time.

"The man says he can take us to a street with several small hotels," Clay soon informed her. "Probably one still has a vacancy. He says they're clean and medium priced. He'd let his sister stay there."

Within five minutes they were idling on a block of respectable three- and four-story buildings while Clay made further inquiries. After the third try, he returned to announce, "One single left, on the top floor."

"Sold," Ashley groaned and dragged herself out of the car.

When her luggage had been carried in, she held her hand out to Clay and they shook. "Thank you for helping like this," she told him. "Do I need to add that I feel awkward and foolish about the whole mess?"

"Think nothing of it," he responded briskly, not quite looking at her.

"I'll let the paper know my plans when I get home."

"No hurry. Hey," he added, shaking his head at her woebegone countenance, "cheer up. After all, you're the first woman in history who ever walked out on Nathan Trent. You should be congratulated."

"Then why don't I feel better about it?" Ashley chafed. "Why do I feel as if it wasn't really my decision?"

"You mean, you feel he *allowed* you to go."

"Something like that." A tedious pause followed, during which the oddity of the situation struck home. Who could have predicted that she would end up depending on Clay and confiding in him after being jilted by Nathan? "I hope you don't mind my asking," she said at last, "but you seem so different from when you arrived. What happened? Was it something I said? Or Nathan?"

Clay chewed the inside of his lip. "Ashley Forrester, inquiring girl. Get a good night's sleep, okay?" And without another word, he turned and went.

The room Clay had found for her was small and clean. It contained an iron bed with a white coverlet, a small round table with a hand-embroidered cloth, an elderly armchair, and, in the corner, a lavatory with two thin towels hanging from a metal bar beside it. Through the open window Ashley could hear pigeons fluttering on the roof and the mewing of one member of Rome's vast cat population. Mechanically she went through her bedtime routine. Because the room was under the roof, it retained much of the day's heat, so she plaited her hair in two braids to keep it off her neck. The last thing she did was hang her blouse by the window to air. All this time her mind was blank.

But as soon as she turned out the rose-shaded overhead light and slipped between the cool, coarse sheets, her thoughts began to whirl. Before she fell asleep, her entire acquaintance with Nathan had passed before her eyes several times. Against her will, she strayed into the land of might-have-been. What if Nathan hadn't gone to Marseilles? Would this be her wedding night? With a pang, she recalled Clay's statement that Nathan's trip had been planned long in advance. But what if Clay and Dominique had not shown up? At this very moment she herself might be lying in Nathan's arms. Or would she? She sat bolt upright. Maybe Nathan had only flown back to Rome to tell her it was over. Why else would he have let her leave with Clay so easily? Easy come, easy go. She could imagine Nathan explaining it that way with a laugh.

She fell back on her pillow, more tired than she had ever been in her life, and soon dreamed of a dark street of hotels that stretched into eternity. She was walking down the street, trying to find a room for the night. But although she could hear people talking and music playing inside every establishment, all the doors were locked and no one answered her knock. Through one window she glimpsed a floor show that featured a woman in an orange dress dancing the can-can. A tall man with black and silver hair sat at a front table applauding. And the biggest and best hotel on the street was the Hotel Sarti.

When she was awakened by chambermaids talking in the hall, Ashley was surprised to find that it was past noon. The square of sky in her window was blue and cloudless. A smell of creosote wafted up from the street. The radio news played in the next room.

Slowly, dreamily, she raised herself on one elbow and yawned delicately against the back of her hand. The pictures in her mind now were of Nathan bursting into her hotel room in Marseilles, his vibrancy filling every corner, and of Nathan finding her on the Palatine Hill. All at once she threw back the covers and jumped out of bed.

"Fool!" she scolded herself aloud. "What are you waiting for? He'll never come again!"

An hour later, dressed in Nathan's blouse and the blue skirt that had been the first thing she saw upon opening her suitcase, she went out to look for a restaurant. Three doors down from her hotel she found a small one. The day's *prezzo fisso* meal, a set menu for a fixed price, was posted on a blackboard near the door. She ordered that because it was the simplest thing to do and spread out her street map and guidebook on the table. After pinpointing her location, she looked up the list of travel agencies and airlines to see if any were within walking distance. A seat on the next plane to University Park was certainly her first order of business. After that, if she had time, she just might see the Trevi Fountain. She wouldn't be seeing it with Nathan at four-thirty, as they had planned, but she couldn't leave Rome without seeing it at all. It would provide a fitting close to her Rome adventure.

Soon she determined that there was a travel bureau only a few blocks away. As she traced with her finger the route she would follow, she came to a street called the Via di Tripoli, which she would have to take for four blocks. Why did the name sound familiar? Was there a museum or an historic church there?

The waiter set before her a small carafe of red table wine, a basket containing several generous chunks of bread, and a shallow plate of minestrone, from which rose a delectable steam. Ashley pushed book and map aside and took up her spoon. *Via di Tripoli.* . . . The soup was hearty and comforting, doubly so because she could not remember when she had last eaten. The wine was robust too, with a pleasant fruitiness hiding in the core of its taste. Slowly Ashley put down her glass. She remembered when she had heard of the Via di Tripoli. It was the street address of the Rome bureau of the *Mediterranean Report*. She would be passing beneath Nathan's windows. Was it fate?

chapter 14

THE ROME BUREAU of the *Mediterranean Report* was on the ground floor of an old but well-preserved office building sandwiched between a new glass-and-chrome bookstore and an old-fashioned pharmacy. The prospect of passing beneath the green canopy that stretched between the door of the office building and the street had kept Ashley loitering before a display of the latest Italian novels in the bookstore window for nearly a minute. The travel bureau stood on the next corner, its gaily postered windows sparkling in the afternoon sun.

A gentleman wearing a gray pinstriped suit and a soft gray fedora came out of the office building and proceeded in the shade of the canopy to a waiting limousine, which slipped smoothly into the stream of traffic like a giant black fish. A young girl in a technician's smock went up the steps carrying a string bag of groceries. Gathering courage, Ashley hitched her shoulder bag higher and walked rapidly toward the travel agency. Passing the *Report* proved to be anticlimactic. The only person in evidence was an office boy of about fifteen, who was looking out the door. The shades of the windows were drawn.

The setback came when she reached the travel agency. A square of white pasteboard taped inside the front door announced the hour at which the agency would reopen, after the customary midday closing. Ashley had been too intent on her own plans to remember the Roman equivalent of siesta time. Stymied, she looked up and down the intersecting streets for a way to pass the next hour. Every place she considered was closed. But she recalled seeing customers in the bookstore, so back she went.

The Rome office of the *Report,* being an outpost of the main office in Marseilles, was not large. A number of brass plates by the door announced that lawyers, a doctor, and an architectural firm also occupied the building. There was, in addition, a painted sign promising fine leather goods upstairs.

When the office boy spoke to her, Ashley realized that she had been standing for too long at the foot of the steps. He was holding the door open for her, assuming that she was a client of someone in the building. Somehow it seemed silly to rush away at that point. Besides, she had not yet bought any leather goods, for which Italy was famous the world over.

"Grazie." She smiled at him as she entered the foyer. To her left was an elevator and an aspidistra in a marble urn. To her right was an open door leading to the offices of the *Report.* A dark-haired girl in a pink dress sat at a desk commanding a view of the foyer, opening mail.

Ashley looked around for an office directory and found none. "The place that sells leather. What floor is it on, please?" she asked the office boy.

He shook his head and mumbled an answer in Italian.

"Just a minute." Ashley fumbled in her purse for her phrase book. She did not deceive herself. Pure curiosity and not the hope of buying gloves had brought her inside. And if Nathan found her outside his door, he would not be deceived either. She moved out of view of the receptionist. But while she was madly searching for the words she needed, and getting nowhere because of her nervousness, the boy went to speak with the receptionist.

"Can I help you?" the girl called out in English.

"No, no, thank you. I'll find it." Ashley nodded, smiled and edged toward the elevator.

"Oh, it's quite all right." The girl came around her desk. "Come in. Which office are you looking for?"

With an unwillingness as great as if she were being asked to walk on hot coals, Ashley entered Nathan's territory. "I was interested in buying some leather goods. Which floor is that?" Her eyes darted in every direction.

"It's the fifth. But they are closed now. It is not long until they open, if you would like to wait here."

"Oh, no. I don't have the time. But thanks, anyway." Ashley started backing out.

"You are American?" the girl asked. "I have been to the States once to visit my brother. He lives in Philadelphia. What city do you live in?"

Curse the girl's friendliness! Ashley answered the question and immediately thereafter could have bitten her tongue.

"I have heard of University Park!" The receptionist was delighted. "It is amazing you are from there."

"Oh, is it?" Ashley managed a weak smile. "Well, I've got to be going. Thanks again for your time."

"Oh, I am not busy now. Almost everyone is out. It is my turn to stay and answer the telephone."

At that moment a door opened behind her and a tall, heavyset woman with iron gray hair done up in a stiff pompadour came out carrying a stack of folders. Ashley guessed she was around sixty.

"Here is someone from University Park," the girl informed the new arrival. "She was looking for Francescato's. Isn't that amazing?"

The woman examined Ashley closely through gold-rimmed glasses. "Yes, indeed. Quite a coincidence." Suddenly she smiled. And the quickness of the smile reminded Ashley of Nathan. "I once lived in University Park. Do you know the Trent family?"

"Everyone has heard of them," Ashley temporized. The sound of footsteps in the foyer made her go cold all over. But they passed by the *Report*.

"Yes, of course. And the beautiful old home. I haven't seen it in several years. It is still in good repair?"

Ashley nodded. "It is, but no one uses it."

The woman clucked her tongue. "Such a pity. It used to be full of life. Parties, dinners, even a dance band for special occasions. I hope it will be reopened someday." She put the folders down on the receptionist's desk and held out a hand. "Allow me to introduce myself. I am Fabiana Sarti."

"You're Miss Sarti?" Ashley gaped at her.

"Why should that surprise you?"

Desperate for an explanation, Ashley confessed, "I've heard of you before, Miss Sarti. To tell you the truth, I work for one of the Trent newspapers."

Miss Sarti stared at Ashley over the rims of her glasses. "My, my, this *is* a coincidence. Well, I must say it's always a pleasure to receive one of our stateside employees, Miss—?"

"I'm Ashley Forrester." Was there a gleam of recognition behind Miss Sarti's spectacles? Ashley couldn't be sure.

"I was just about to have a cup of tea, Miss Forrester, to brace me up for the afternoon. Won't you join me?"

"Oh, no, I couldn't possibly," Ashley fluttered, utterly horrified. "What I mean to say is, it's very kind of you, but I wouldn't want to impose on your working hours. Besides, I still have shopping to do and not much time. I'm on my way back to the States, you understand." Her mind flew back to the day when Nathan had discovered her in Charles LeSueur's office in Marseilles. If he found her here, too, his rage would know no bounds. He would think she was still snooping around for a story.

Miss Sarti fixed Ashley in an imperious glare. "But my dear, the shops are closed and the heat is dreadful at this hour. Surely you can spare a few minutes to humor an old woman? I would like to hear more about University Park."

Chastened, Ashley replied, "Of course, Miss Sarti. It will be my pleasure." Feeling like a lamb being led to slaughter, she followed Miss Sarti into her office.

"Giuliana," Miss Sarti stopped to say, "please see that we are not disturbed." And she closed the door.

Miss Sarti's office was small but handsomely furnished. In addition to the cluster of filing cabinets and bookshelves that surrounded her desk, there was a glass-topped coffee table and three leather armchairs to one side. These, Ashley comprehended with a shock, were for people waiting to see Nathan. The door to the left of Miss Sarti's desk bore an Italian word that Ashley guessed meant "chief" or "director."

"Won't you sit down?" Miss Sarti motioned to the armchairs. To the tray of tea things on the edge of her desk she added another cup and saucer, then carried it to the table. "Now then," she said with satisfaction. "Do you take milk or sugar? No? I became very fond of tea when I was studying in England, but I don't often have the chance to enjoy it with a new friend."

"Have you worked for Trent Enterprises a long time?" Ashley asked politely, keenly aware that she was being accorded special treatment. Miss Sarti was not the sort to put aside her work for every visiting fireman.

"It's hard to remember a time before Trent Enterprises," Miss Sarti answered, stirring her tea. "My father and the present Mr. Trent's grandfather were friends. I have been personal secretary to three generations of Trents. So of course part of my life has been spent in the old home place in University Park. Now, however, I spend much of my time in this office, because I am Italian by background. One-half executive and one-half maid-of-all-work," she explained with a twinkle.

"You must know Trent Enterprises better than just about anybody," Ashley ventured to say. She kept her eyes on the door to Nathan's office.

Miss Sarti was pleased. "In a way, I do. Young Mr. Trent calls me the auntie of the company. Sometimes I feel more like its grandmother, when I think of how many changes I've seen over the years. But Trent Enterprises is in good hands. Mr. Nathan is committed to the same high standards as was his grandfather."

"So I've heard." Ashley decided that she liked Miss Sarti. There was warmth behind the formal manner. But she was not prepared for the woman's next remark.

"My only worry is what will happen to Trent Enterprises in the next generation," said Miss Sarti. "There is no heir."

Ashley sipped her tea. The silence was deafening. "The present Mr. Trent is not old," she said finally. "Perhaps there will be."

Miss Sarti shook her head gravely. "I'm afraid he will not marry now."

"Now?" Ashley asked faintly.

"He was to be married this week," Miss Sarti ruminated, "and a happier man I've never seen. But something has gone wrong and it seems to be over. I was looking forward to meeting the girl who had made him so happy. From his description of her, she was—is—thoroughly charming."

Ashley stirred her tea unnecessarily. She knew she was blushing to the roots of her hair. Miss Sarti's revelations amounted to a breach of business etiquette. One did not discuss the boss's personal life with an underling and a stranger. Yet Ashley had the feeling that Miss Sarti knew exactly what she was doing.

"Even if one has a son," Ashley said carefully, "there is no guarantee that he will follow in his father's footsteps. If Mr. Trent is marrying only to ensure the continuation of Trent Enterprises, then he may be setting himself up for a big disappointment."

"Oh, that isn't his intention. It is *my* prerogative to worry about an heir—as 'auntie' of Trent Enterprises," Miss Sarti corrected her quite merrily. "Mr. Trent has had no other thought in his mind but spending his life with the woman he loves." She removed her glasses and polished them on a lace handkerchief. "But I am rambling on and you haven't much time. Forgive me, Miss Forrester. And I myself have work to do, since Mr. Trent is in Rome this week and wants all sorts of things done immediately."

"Then I mustn't stay." With a stricken glance at the door of Nathan's office, Ashley set down her cup and prepared to rise.

"Heavens, I didn't mean that we couldn't finish our tea. Please keep you seat. Besides, Mr. Trent isn't in at the moment. He cancelled all his appointments for the day."

To drown his sorrows with Dominique, Ashley brooded.

"Now let's see," Miss Sarti continued. "We haven't talked about University Park yet. I used to have friends there. Do you know . . . ?"

For several minutes they spoke of mutual acquaintances and of Creighton University, while Ashley grew more and more restive. Even though Nathan was supposed to be elsewhere, every noise outside seemed to herald his approach. It would have been difficult to face him without having Miss Sarti's remarks to consider. Now, it would be impossible. She desperately wanted a few minutes to herself and could barely concentrate on Miss Sarti's questions. When the telephine jangled, she jumped like a startled rabbit.

"I'll only be a moment," Miss Sarti said, and went to answer it.

From the coffee table Ashley picked up the latest issue of the *Mediterranean Report* and tried to interest herself in an analysis of Italian political parties. But as soon as she heard the voice speaking to Miss Sarti, faint though it was, the words swam on the page. It was Nathan.

For a good five minutes Miss Sarti read a stack of accumulated messages to her employer, pausing to take down instructions after each. The last one caused Ashley to abandon the magazine entirely.

"Your friend Alfredo called at eleven-thirty," Miss Sarti informed him. "He has the guest list I sent. But now, in view of the—" and here Miss Sarti hesitated discreetly "—*recent developments,* he wonders if you still want to give the dinner at his restaurant. He's perfectly willing to do it, but thinks perhaps it should be postponed even later. Out of consideration for *her* feelings. What? No, he says the final decision is yours. Yes, yes, I agree. That's certainly preferable. Then shall I see about it? Fine."

So Alfredo knew where Dominique spent the night, yet he was still willing to stage a dinner party for Nathan? Ashley shook her head in disbelief. She would never, ever, understand them.

"As for your other appointment this afternoon," Miss Sarti said, as her eyes came to rest briefly on Ashley, "I feel almost certain that the other party will be there, so do make an effort to show up. How do I know? Just trust me, Mr. Trent. Am I ever wrong?" She laughed at his answer and then went on, "I've had an interesting visitor this afternoon. In fact—"

Ashley was on her feet, waving her arms urgently. "No!" she whispered. "Don't mention me! Don't tell him I'm here! Please!"

"Oh, never mind," Miss Sarti improvised. "It can wait until later." She squinted at the wall clock. "Will you be coming in before that last appointment? You're where? That's quite a distance away. You'll have to hurry to make it, won't you? Yes, I understand. Then I'll go ahead with the arrangements we discussed. And I'll send a telegram to let you know. *Ciao.*" She replaced the receiver and folded her hands on her desk. "Might I ask, Miss Forrester, why you didn't want Mr. Trent to know you were here? Have the two of you met, by any chance?"

"I once tried to interview him for my newspaper," Ashley said truthfully, "and the experience didn't turn out well for either of us. I'm sure he wouldn't want me to be here."

"Then your visit shall remain just between us," Miss Sarti promised, but she did not look convinced by Ashley's explanation.

"I really have to go now," Ashley said firmly, taking up her shoulder bag. "I've enjoyed meeting you. And thanks for the tea."

Miss Sarti accompanied Ashley to the door. "You're flying back tonight?"

"Maybe I'll take a train as far as Paris," Ashley replied. "I have to go to a travel agency and decide. That's why I'm in the neighborhood."

"Not to see the Trevi Fountain? It's only a few streets away. Or perhaps you have already seen it."

"No, I haven't. Actually, I was saving it until the end." Ashley looked at her wristwatch and was interested to see that Miss Sarti was checking the wall clock again. It was ten minutes after four.

"Oh, you must see it," Miss Sarti urged. "And don't forget to toss in a coin."

"Yes," Ashley returned, "I will. I promised myself that I would visit the Trevi Fountain today."

Miss Sarti gave a significant nod. "It's a promise worth keeping, Miss Forrester. It is much more important than visiting the leather shop. Good-bye now. And good luck."

chapter 15

AT TWENTY-EIGHT MINUTES past four Ashley reached the
end of the Via di S. Vincenzo and saw the Trevi Fountain.
Spanning the tiny piazza, it seemed to fill every inch of
space to the sky with baroque detail.

Hot and breathless from running half of the distance,
she took a handkerchief from her shoulder bag, dabbed
it with cologne, and blotted her temples and throat. She
had run straight past the travel agency without stopping.

A score of sightseers in ones and twos milled about
the blue-green basin in front of the fountain or sat along
a semicircular stone bench facing it. To one side stood
a compact group of camera-bedecked Japanese tourists,
listening to a tour guide. Through this crowd of strangers
the life of the neighborhood patiently threaded itself. No
figure among the throng was familiar to Ashley. But it
was only twenty-nine minutes past four.

She crossed the street and positioned herself before
the center of the fountain, in order to admire its symmetry
as much as her preoccupied state would allow. It was a
wall fountain, built into the back of a former private
residence called the Palazzo Poli, the windows and pi-
lasters of which framed the massed rocks and figures of
the water tableau. A statue of Neptune commanded the
central niche, flanked by feminine figures representing
Health and Abundance. The sea god was also attended
by two tritons, half man and half fish, leading horses—
the one symbolizing the calm ocean and the other the
stormy ocean. Below and around all of these, over an

artful arrangement of naturalistically carved rocks, cascaded the waters of the Acqua Vergine Antica, one of the six aqueducts that slake the thirst of Rome.

It was four-thirty.

With infinite slowness Ashley wheeled in a complete circle, scanning the face of every passerby and all the windows that fronted on the little square. The sight of an approaching taxi made her heart skip a beat, but she soon saw that it contained only a woman and a child. When she faced the fountain once more, she asked herself if she had been wrong. Had she misread the signals?

She took a seat before the shallow pool that the fountain served. The bottom of the basin glittered with coins. Within the space of a minute half a dozen more had been added, tossed over the shoulders of self-conscious tourists.

Again she looked around her. Nested like Chinese boxes, her most precious hopes lay hidden deep within her. And her innermost, her most treasured hope, was that Nathan would keep their appointment at the Trevi Fountain. She had believed he would, without until now actually admitting it to herself, throughout the adversities of the past twenty-four hours. Meeting Miss Sarti, and thus discovering how completely she, Ashley, had misinterpreted Dominique's remarks about Nathan's secretary, had only increased that hope. So had Miss Sarti's references to the "last appointment" that Nathan was to keep that afternoon. But now she had to face the possibility that he might never have intended to come. Her hand went to the silk rose at her bosom and she touched the tear-stained petal with a fingertip. She had worn the blouse today for him.

Suddenly a flurry of activity broke out practically under her feet. A street urchin, bent on scooping up a

handful of coins without being seen by a nearby policeman, leaned over too far and fell into the pool. The
policeman came running, and the boy scampered to the
other side and away, splashing several onlookers in the
process. Cameras clicked, people laughed and exclaimed, and a general roar went up when one of the
gamin's cohorts, taking advantage of the policeman's
distraction, filched a handful of money from another part
of the fountain and fled down a side street. The next
time Ashley checked the hour, it was a quarter to five.

An old woman in black shuffled up to the fountain
and filled a tin pitcher from it, just as people had been
doing there since the building of the aqueducts. Ordi-
narily Ashley would have snapped up such a bit of local
color for use in one of her newspaper stories. But today
all she could think of was that Nathan was not coming.
How could she ever have imagined he would?

She rose to her feet and took three coins from her
billfold. They would be her good-bye to Italy. How did
the saying go? The first coin ensures your return to Rome.
She closed her eyes, tossed, and heard it strike the water.
She studied the two remaining pieces in her palm. One
was for a husband and the other for luck in love. And
what did she care about either now? She dropped them
back in her bag and shut the clasp.

From somewhere behind her two coins arced past,
winking in the sun, and hit the water together.

"If you're going to wish, wish for everything you
can," said a deep, well-known voice.

And there he was, not ten feet away, standing a little
crooked as he always did, and smiling a lopsided smile.
In the street stood a red sports car, the driver's door ajar.

"The traffic," he said, his eyes caressing her.

"Oh." She started toward him, weak with relief. "It

doesn't matter. You're here." She smiled. "Do you want to sit here awhile?"

"No, let's go." He held out his hand.

She stopped halfway to him. "Where? To the embassy?" she asked, when all she wanted to do was to fling herself into his arms.

"No, no embassy for us."

Then he'd meant what he said about not marrying her. There were to be no wedding plans. A bittersweet peace filled her. So be it. Then he could have her on his terms. She didn't care anymore. She only knew she couldn't bear to leave him again. She went up to him and clasped his hand.

"All right," she said. "Let's go."

Nathan swept her into his embrace, his face glowing with a strong emotion. "I knew you would be here," he said, swinging her around so exuberantly that her feet left the ground.

Caught between joy and confusion, as she had been since the day they had met, she suppressed both by teasing, "You would have made such a good Caesar."

"I've always thought so," he agreed grinning, "but why do *you* think so?"

"'I came, I saw, I conquered.' That's the way you do things."

"I'm not through conquering you," he said with a deliberate leer. "And there's another Latin phrase I like even better: *Carpe diem*—'seize the day.' In other words, we're wasting time here."

"I wasn't even sure you would waste time on showing up," Ashley returned in her same coy manner. "I heard that you cancelled all your appointments today."

"You wouldn't by any chance be the 'interesting visitor' who showed up at the *Report* this afternoon?" Nathan grinned down at her.

"Why *did* you cancel your appointments?" she persisted, when all she wanted was for him to kiss her. "Need to catch up on your sleep?"

"You can do better than that," Nathan told her. "Say what's on your mind. Ask me point-blank. You're a reporter."

"Did you spend the night with Dominique?" The words fell like live grenades into the waning afternoon.

"Dominique?" Nathan repeated. "Sleep with her? Darling, I didn't even see her."

Ashley leaned back against his encircling arms and looked into his sunlit face. "Why didn't you see her? Because the lights were out?"

"I didn't see her, Madame Prosecutor, because I didn't go up to my room. After you and Clay left, I telephoned Alfredo from the lobby and told him where she was. He was there to collect her in fifteen minutes. Then the fireworks began. You didn't hear the hotel explode?"

"You have all the answers, don't you, Mr. Trent?" she asked archly.

"I have to. I keep running into this lady reporter who's full of questions. Especially questions about my character." He reached for her hands and placed one on each of his shoulders. Then his own hands clasped her waist loosely.

"I thought you didn't like publicity," Ashley reminded him. "Aren't you afraid the paparazzi will come by and snap our picture? Here we are in broad daylight."

"I'm with the prettiest woman in Rome," Nathan said. "Let them."

She smoothed his collar and tried not to look pleased. Some instinct for self-protection made her keep fighting his charm.

"Any more questions?" he demanded sardonically.

"Then Alfredo and Dominique are back together?"

she asked and laughed, because she really could not stop being inquisitive.

Nathan laughed too and replied, "They were never really apart. But they'd been fighting for months about the long hours Alfredo was putting in at the restaurant. Dominique felt neglected. To get back at him, she accepted a singing engagement an hour's drive from Rome. When Alfredo merely congratulated her, she was furious."

"She never wanted to go. She just wanted him to beg her not to," Ashley deduced.

"Right. But Alfredo didn't catch on."

"Men." Ashley sighed, and laced her fingers behind his neck. "And so poor Dominique was driven to the desperate measure of jumping in your bed."

"Women," Nathan said with equal sarcasm.

"But don't expect me to believe Dominique was only interested in getting Alfredo's attention," Ashley contended. "She fully intended to enjoy her night with you."

"As if I had no plans of my own," Nathan drawled. "But she's volatile. I doubt she really thought the whole thing through."

"That's what they all say. Afterward," Ashley retorted.

"You're a cynical little thing. Is it your profession?"

"It's the people I meet," she returned pointedly.

Nathan pulled her closer. "Do you know something?" he asked, a wicked sparkle in his eyes.

"What?"

"I don't want to talk about Alfredo and Dominique."

"Neither do I," said Ashley, as the last of her resistance to him dissipated. She tilted up her mouth to meet his kiss.

"We'd better go," Nathan said finally, "before we do become a public spectacle."

In the car, just before he switched on the ignition, he reached over and turned her face toward his. "Why so serious? It's a little late for regrets. In fact, I won't allow them."

"What? Oh, no, no regrets," Ashley said evenly. "None at all." And she even managed to smile.

In a matter of minutes Ashley's luggage had been retrieved from her hotel and they were on their way out of Rome. At one point, when a sleek passenger train rocketed by, she remarked, "I was planning to take a train to Paris and fly home from there," hoping this news would make him reveal his intentions. He had not said a word about where they were going.

But Nathan only replied calmly, "All your plans have been cancelled, I'm afraid. I'm doing the planning now."

He drove skillfully, even with flair, and they were soon out of congested Rome, heading southwest to the coast. Ashley divided her time between taking in the scenery and wondering where they were going. She tried not to look at him very often, lest he realize that she could not get enough of the sight of him. It was like basking in sunlight to be near him, and she had the impulse to store up as much sunlight as she could, before he went out of her life again.

At the coast they turned north. As if settling himself for a long drive, Nathan loosened his tie and shrugged off his jacket. His hand fell on her knee, patted it in a casually possessive way, and stayed there.

She did not quite have the courage to ask their immediate plans, but there were plenty of other questions to try. "What happened between you and Clay after I left?" she wanted to know.

"A lot." With a glance her way, he added, "I was surprised to see him. To put it mildly."

"So was I." Ashley turned to him, her face imploring.

"I know what you must have thought when you saw us together. You thought you had been right from the beginning, didn't you? That I was part of a plan of revenge or some cruel joke. The minute you turned your back, there Clay was with me. I know it looked bad. But I really—"

She was stilled by the pressure of his hand on her knee. "All of that crossed my mind when I saw you two," he said. "I admit it. But I got over it pretty fast. After all, I know you a lot better than I did when I made those accusations in Marseilles. Our time together counted for something." Gratified, Ashley said nothing more and Nathan continued, "Clay was on his way to meet friends in Dubrovnik for a vacation."

"He told me he came to Rome just for me," Ashley confessed quietly. "I should have known better than to believe him."

"He thought he could kill two birds with one stone. It's a sport Clay excels at," Nathan observed without heat.

"But later, in the taxi, I thought he had changed his mind about wanting me to go back with him," Ashley went on, groping for an explanation. "It was as if . . . as if I were off limits to him then."

Nathan winked at her. He patted her knee again. "Let's talk about it tonight."

"And where will we be tonight?"

"Together."

The sports car sped along, weaving in and out of the lengthening shadows, caressing the curves of the road. They talked of other things—the mountains, the sea, where Shelley died, the quarries of Carrara marble to the north of them, and Napoleon's exile on the Isle of Elba.

Occasionally, when a villa flashed by, or a terrace of

olive trees, Ashley would say, "Jean would like that. I wish she could see it."

"Do you know how often you mention her?" Nathan asked.

"No, do I? Well, I suppose it's only natural. She's my closest family. And she was good to me," Ashley added, thinking to herself that she now faced the dreary prospect of telling Jean for the second time that she wasn't getting married after all.

At nightfall they turned inland a few miles and soon entered a hilly village that seemed to have been forgotten by time not long after it was carved out of the white stone of the mountainside. At the first cross street, the car had to nose its way through a herd of goats. The lights were intermittent and dim in the narrow, crooked streets, but Nathan found his way surely to a street even more narrow than the rest, which seemed to rise up the mountain perpendicular to the village. It led to a stone inn with a slanting red tile roof, recently constructed but possessing the grace of age. When Ashley stepped out under the portico, the wind smelled of pine.

Unobtrusive staff members disappeared with car and luggage.

"Here we are," Nathan said. He took her arm and they climbed the front steps.

At the door, Ashley hung back. "Are we making a long trip? Or is this our destination?"

"It won't be as long as I would like it to be," Nathan answered after a moment's hesitation. "Our time is limited." He flashed his quick smile. "We'll have to make every minute count."

"Carpe diem, is that the phrase? Make hay while the sun shines?" she asked breezily.

"While the moon shines." He winked.

Ashley turned her head aside to hide her emotion. She need not have bothered, for Nathan had already sauntered ahead to speak with the bearded man at the desk, who seemed to be expecting them.

chapter 16

"THIS GENTLEMAN TELLS me that a specialty of the house is being served tonight," Nathan said to Ashley when he had finished at the registration desk. "It's wild boar, and they've just taken it off the spit. Does that tempt you? It's past dinner time."

"Yes, I'm starving. Let's go to the dining room now. As long as someone else is taking the luggage to our rooms, there's no need to go up," Ashley said quickly, but not quickly enough to keep Nathan from raising an eyebrow.

"*Rooms?*" he repeated ironically. "Two of them? Somehow I don't think we need more than one now."

"Of course," Ashley stammered, nonplussed. "Which way is the dining room?" Then she saw that it was straight ahead, in plain sight, and hurried toward it in an agony of embarrassment.

But Nathan caught up with her easily in three strides and said over her shoulder, "Relax. We're not strangers, you know. I seem to recall becoming acquainted in Rome."

The truth was that she did feel singularly shy about the prospect of sharing a night with him. Ever since they had left Rome, there had been suspense in the air and the sensation of beginning all over again for her. It was almost as if they had never made love before. She suspected that Nathan felt it too, but his manner was so remote, so confidently masterful, that she could not be certain. There was only a slight increase in the courtliness of his treatment of her, which might suggest that he felt a change in their relationship. At any rate, while she grew more nervous by the minute, he was enjoying himself thoroughly. She wanted to put off going upstairs as long as possible.

The dining room was lit by oil lamps on each table and by an open fire appropriate to the coolness of the higher altitude. Nathan asked for and was given a table by one of the front windows, overlooking the scattered lights of the village.

"This is beautiful. Have you been here many times?" Ashley asked.

"Only once. I stumbled across it last year. Just one of the many little places I want to experience again, with you," he replied smoothly, gallantly.

The old need to resist his charisma welled up in her. "I hope your trip to Marseilles was a success."

"A problem came up that had to be handled immediately. I would have preferred to put it off a few days and deal with it Friday, when I have to be in Marseilles anyway for an annual meeting. But that wasn't possible." The waiter came and Nathan considered the menu with him, asking several questions. Ashley concentrated on lining up her silverware with the edge of the table. That took care of Clay's insinuations about the necessity of the Marseilles trip. She was relieved, but she was also disgusted with herself for continuing to check up on Nathan.

When Nathan returned to the conversation, he was eerily in tune with her thoughts. "You and I both know that Clay has his good points. He wouldn't have become my friend—or your fiancé—without having some admirable qualities."

"That's true." Ashley was noticing the other, obviously affluent, diners, the fire, the stuccoed ceiling with exposed beams, and the pervasive aroma of wood smoke and sizzling meat. She had to admit that Nathan could pick the settings for his rendezvous. But of course, he had had plenty of practice.

"And leaving Trent Enterprises is a smart move," Nathan was saying. "Clay's always wondered if he got his breaks on his own or because he was my friend. Now he doesn't have to worry about that. He can go as far as he wants in his new career and know that the top spot isn't already taken by me. You see," Nathan concluded, "Clay's problems began long before he knew me. I was merely the embodiment of everything he aspired to, and that made him envious to a dangerous degree."

"But you've sorted everything out between you?"

"Yes, everything," Nathan replied, giving particular weight to the last word.

A salad platter and bread arrived, soon followed by slices of the roasted boar with all the trimmings. Lulled by the warmth of the room and the excellent meal, Ashley began to grow comfortable in the aura of mystery that still surrounded their journey. Nathan's every glance and gesture seemed calculated to make her feel protected and cherished. At least, she mused, this time together would be pleasant, however short. Nathan, as Dominique had noted, was a gentleman.

They were lingering over coffee when he raised her hand to his lips and kissed each fingertip one at a time. "I'm thinking of opening the house in University Park," he remarked, watching her attentively across the lamp's glow. "It would be nice to have it waiting for trips to the States. What do you think?"

"Does it matter what I think?" She was puzzled.

"It needs some renovating—and I'd appreciate a woman's advice."

Their knees touched and Ashley suppressed a shiver.

"I see," she said. "You'll be visiting there sometime to see about the house and you want me to look it over with you."

"That's what I said."

She looked out the window. "I may not be at the *Chronicle* when you get around to that, so don't count on my help. I'm looking for another job."

"Oh?" He was clasping her hand across the table now, his thumb stroking her palm. "Did Clay put this idea in your head?"

She tried to pull her hand away, but he held it firmly. "Of course not. It has nothing to do with his offer. I told you in Marseilles that I was thinking of making a change before I came to Europe. Now, more than ever, I know it's time for me to move on. Both for professional reasons and because—" she made herself look at him "—because I have to answer the question for myself, 'Is there life after Nathan Trent?' When this little interlude is over and I go back to the States, I don't want to work for you anymore, even if I never see you. I don't want to be reminded—"

Nathan winced. "Darling, there's so much you don't understand."

"None of it matters since we won't be seeing each other after this," Ashley interrupted him hurriedly. "I'm sorry I brought up the subject. I didn't mean to spoil the evening."

A waiter came to give Nathan a message.

"There's a phone call for me," he said. "I've been expecting it. Finish your coffee and I'll be back in just a minute. Then we're going to talk more about these plans of yours."

When he returned, she had not moved. "Shall we talk upstairs?" he asked, regarding her in a penetrating way that made her think he knew something about her she didn't know herself.

"Yes," she said, meaning no.

"Are you tired?" His arm went around her as she stood up.

"Not particularly. Just nervous," she said without thinking.

"Nervous about what?"

"Not exactly nervous, I guess. I feel like . . ." a bride. A blushing bride on her wedding night, she had almost said. "Maybe I am tired after all," she finished with a tremulous smile.

Their room was on the second floor, which they reached by means of a broad staircase of rough-hewn timbers. Their luggage stood inside the door in a close row and looked oddly intimate together, her suitcases of pale blue beside his tan leather one. Across the room on a bedside table stood a vase containing a single dusty-pink rose, the twin of the one on Ashley's blouse.

"Yes," said Nathan, surveying the scene drolly, "I think one room will be enough."

He shut the door and drew her into his arms. His kisses were hard and hungry and she was not at all prepared for them. She tried to turn her head away, but he caught her by the hair and forced her lips to remain under his.

"Wait. Please," she moaned.

"I *have* waited. All day."

"No, let me—" But he covered her mouth again, and her lips were expertly parted by his tongue. His other hand pulled her blouse out of her skirt and slipped inside the waistband of her panties. She tried to get away, stumbling backward. Nathan pinned her against the wall.

"What's the matter?" he demanded roughly. "We're

just picking up where we left off. Or have you forgotten?"

"I haven't forgotten," she breathed in a hoarse whisper, rolling her head this way and that as his repeated kisses lit a pool of fire in the hollow of her throat. The hand inside her clothing moved lower. "But so much has happened since then," she cried. "I need time, I need—"

With an exclamation Nathan tore away the silk rose. The fickle top button of her blouse sprang open with it. Ashley moaned again as his hand slid in to cup her breast. Her body was not her own. It belonged to Nathan and it was calling out to him, tempting him, begging to be displayed and enjoyed. The sinuous spiral of ecstasy had begun.

He pulled her abruptly away from the wall, crushing her into him, so that she felt his readiness and arched herself to meet it, unable to hold herself back. But numbly she thought: I can't go through with it. It means so much to me and so little to him.... He was unfastening her skirt when she cried out for him to stop.

After that it was deathly still. Nathan flung himself away from her, stopping in the center of the room with his back to her. With trembling fingers, Ashley rebuttoned her blouse.

"Sorry," he threw over his shoulder, knifelike. "Assault isn't my style. You were willing enough in Rome, little lady."

Mortified, she ducked her head. "I still am."

"You have one hell of a way of showing it," he rapped. Then his tone softened. "What's wrong? Do you want to talk about it?"

The spacious bed was covered by a heavy fringed bedspread, perhaps hand-woven, in an intricate design of black and cream. Instead of answering him, Ashley skirted the edge of it and reached for the rose in its vase. She inhaled its innocent sweetness. While she was doing this, Nathan stalked over to the drapes and drew back one pair, revealing a balcony behind a sliding door.

"You had the rose put here, didn't you?" she asked.

"Yes, I did. You've always reminded me of roses."

Ashley set the vase down carefully. "You're very good at planning this sort of evening, aren't you?" she challenged, but without rancor. "Down to the last perfect detail."

He was lounging against the doorjamb, taking off his tie and unbuttoning his cuffs. His coat hung across the back of a chair. "Is that what this is to you?"

"Of course. Isn't that what it is to you?" she returned unsteadily.

"Come out on the balcony," he suggested, turning away. "There's a moon tonight."

She went as far as the threshold and looked out. The balcony faced the steep slope behind the inn. A million stars and a crescent moon softly illuminated the craggy summit. A cricket orchestra sawed away in the grass. Somewhere a cowbell tinkled. Nathan stood by the railing. The breeze ruffled his hair and molded his shirt and pants to his handsome body. A handsome stranger.

"I'm cold," she lied. "Maybe I should stay in here."

"Suit yourself." His even white teeth, gleaming out of the shadows, seemed to bite off the words.

"Please don't be angry with me, Nathan."

"I'm not angry. Impatient, maybe. Why don't you take a hot bath if you're cold? I know you like to do that, as do all sensuous women. You are very sensuous, you know, when you let yourself be."

She wished she could see his face, but hoped he could not see hers. His voice revealed nothing of his present feelings. "Yes, maybe I'll do that."

"There's champagne on the way," he added.

"What are we toasting?" She tried to sound festive and failed dismally.

"We'll decide that when the champagne arrives."

"Wait a minute." She went to her suitcase, unwrapped the two silver goblets and took them out on the balcony, where she handed them to Nathan. "Here. We can use these."

"Very nice." He held them up to the light from the doorway. "Where did you get them?"

Ashley shrugged jerkily. "I bought them for a wedding gift."

"For whom?"

"For us. The day after we talked about getting married. Do you recall that too?" she dared to ask.

"I do."

"But why not use them anyway?" she went on, bright and brittle. "No use in saving them, is there?"

"None at all," he agreed a trifle huskily. As she started to go, he said, "Ashley, considering your view of this whole situation, why did you come along?"

"I didn't have the strength to say no," she replied simply. "I love you."

Leaving Nathan to his contemplations, she unpacked her robe and nightgown and took them into the bathroom. A large, squarish tub was built into an alcove to one side. As she ran hot water, she heard Nathan leave the balcony and answer a knock at the door. Following this, while she undressed and pinned up her hair, she heard voices and a crunch of ice, as the bucket of champagne was carried in and set down. She tested the water with her toe and let herself down into it. The tub was long enough to stretch out in and she did so thankfully, resting her head against the slope of the back. She listened to the sounds of Nathan undressing—keys and change landing on a table top, his suitcase being unsnapped, a drawer opening and shutting. Even the unbuckling of his belt was audible. He started to whistle *Yes, Sir, That's My Baby*.

Ashley inhaled the steam that had turned the whole room foggy, and closed her eyes tightly. She could not bear such an intensely intimate situation. Because what would happen tomorrow? Wouldn't he put her on the train to Paris with a wave and a smile? Or would that come the day after? As efficient as he was, he had probably already bought her a one-way ticket all the way to University Park.

In the bedroom a cork popped and ricocheted. The champagne gurgled once, twice.

There was a rap at the bathroom door.

"Yes?" She sat up, wrapping her arms around her knees.

Nathan entered carrying the two goblets, brimming. He was wearing only a black towel wrapped tightly about his hips. She scooted lower in the water, as if it afforded some cover.

With all the poise in the world, Nathan sat down on the edge of the tub and handed her a goblet. He raised his own. "I'm the persistent one, remember? And the night is very long. To us."

She drank, eyeing him over the edge of her cup. One instant she wanted to blurt out a thousand thoughts and feelings that had been building up inside her all afternoon. The next, she could hardly remember her name.

"What are you thinking?" he asked, brushing a trailing curl back behind her ear. And suddenly, with that tender gesture, he became once more the Nathan she knew, the

Nathan that some part of her had always known—not a stranger briefly encountered in a foreign country.

She said what was in her heart. "Why did you let me go with Clay when I wanted so much to stay?"

"Clay came to Rome to play a game," Nathan replied, stroking the line of her jaw with intoxicating gentleness. "No holds barred and winner take all. I refused to play. That's all."

"Why?"

He leaned over and took her chin in his hand. His eyes strayed over her body with great leisure and came reluctantly back to her face. "Because it wasn't a game to me. Don't you see how it would have tarnished what we meant to each other to defend it to Clay, point by point? Do you think I wanted to win you the way a horse-trader acquires a mare, simply by outsmarting the other fellow? What does that have to do with love?"

"So that's why you didn't try to defend yourself or me against the things Clay was saying," Ashley realized.

With a twinkle in his eye, Nathan picked up a bar of soap and began to rub it over her knees, which were still drawn up under her chin. He went on talking as if nothing were happening, as if he had no idea of the wanton desires his touch was bringing to life inside her.

"That's right. And besides, I wanted you to hear everything Clay had to say. So that if you did decide to go with him, you'd know exactly what you were getting."

Her eyes widened in disbelief. "Nathan Trent, how could you ever imagine such a thing? Is *that* why you insisted I leave the hotel with him?"

"You and I are a lot alike," Nathan told her. He splashed water on her and ran his hand down her calves to smooth away the lather. "You once said that you couldn't give half of yourself to anyone, that you had to give all or nothing. And I can't take half of you either. I want all of you or I want you out of my life. That's why I gave you that last chance to choose."

"It was so easy for you," Ashley reproached him, but she was barely able to follow the conversation. He had picked up the soap again and was looking her over wickedly.

"It may have looked easy, but my jealousy almost got the better of me," Nathan corrected her gruffly.

"You? Jealous on my account?"

"Furiously jealous." His nostrils flared. "Letting you go was as much a test of my self-control as it was of yours and Clay's. I nearly came after you."

Ashley sat up and flung her arms around his waist. "What did you say at the taxi? You didn't threaten him, did you?"

"No. That was the hardest part. I only told him to see that you found a place to stay. Where—and with whom—I left up to the two of you. Of course by then," his voice deepened ominously, "Clay knew better than to interfere."

"You might not have been playing his game," Ashley said with a smile, "but you were gambling all the same. Did you know how much the odds were in your favor?"

"Yes." He grinned. "That's why I came to the Trevi." He soaped her shoulders. The smell of sandalwood filled her head. When he touched the sensitive spot at the nape of her neck, she let her head fall back against his hand with a little shudder and her lips parted in a silent moan.

"You didn't come to the Trevi because Miss Sarti urged you to?" she teased him languidly.

"So you *were* at the office." Nathan laughed. "And she managed to mention the fountain to you as well? Don't tell me we're only puppets worked by the redoubtable Fabiana. She's been trying to get me to settle down for years, and you walked right into her trap."

"You know we're not." With her arms still around his waist, Ashley rested her cheek against his thigh and felt the muscles tense. "I came because somehow I knew you would be there, in spite of everything that happened with Clay and Dominique. Mmmmm," she moaned, as Nathan massaged her back with a strong, sure motion. "But I might not have made it. I considered not going. What if I hadn't?"

"Then I would have been right to let you leave with Clay," he said, bending over her to massage lower and lower, causing ripples in the water that, breaking against her body, set up ripples of passion in her skin.

"Marriage itself isn't that important," she said. "I don't care about a piece of paper or being made an honest woman, for heaven's sake. I just don't want to leave you. Ever."

Nathan put her goblet in her hand. "You've hardly touched your champagne," he said.

She raised her head lazily and took a sip. Then, watching the bubbles rise, she had no qualms about asking, "Where do we go from here? What happens tomorrow?"

"I thought you'd never ask, you timid creature. We're on our way to Marseilles. Hotels are fine, but it's time to go home. To our home, Ashley. I made most of the arrangements after my business meeting yesterday. By the time we arrive the house should be ready for its new mistress to—" He broke off to chide her, "Are you listening? You seem desperately interested in your champagne all of a sudden."

She was reaching to the bottom of the cup, where something glittered that was not bubbles. She lifted out the ring and held it up in astonishment. Nathan took it from her and slipped it on her finger. It was a square-cut emerald in an antique setting surrounded by diamonds.

He spread her hand out on his scarred knee. "Like it?"

"It's the most beautiful ring in the world."

"And there's something else," he went on. "That phone call I received tonight was to let me know when your stepmother would be arriving in Marseilles."

"Jean? Coming here? But why?"

"Despite the lack of interest in marriage you just expressed," Nathan said with playful sternness, "I'm going to marry you. And I wanted you to have family there. My impression is that you and Jean care for each other. She certainly wants to come."

"You talked with her?"

"Yes, I did. Strangely enough, she had already heard something about me."

"You wonderful, wonderful man."

"I know." Nathan laughed. "Miss Sarti has gone on ahead to meet Jean and entertain her in case we're delayed. Since we're starting our honeymoon now, we may have trouble sticking to a schedule." With a devilish grin of determination, he took up the soap again and began rhythmically to soap her breasts.

"I hope Miss Sarti doesn't know what we're doing!" Ashley protested, with a gasp of pure pleasure.

"She'll be too busy fluttering over the details of the wedding to think about the principal actors. I trust you don't mind if she handles it. She's been waiting for years." Nathan chuckled. He bent to kiss her, his hand still moving in the seductive rhythm. "Do you see now why I couldn't throw a marriage proposal into Clay's little contest, to top his job offer to you? You might always have wondered whether I did it just to get the better of Clay instead of because I couldn't live without you."

"Is there anything else you haven't told me?" Ashley murmured between kisses.

"Oh, lots of things," Nathan growled. "Enough to keep us talking for a lifetime. A marathon interview."

"That's right," she said dreamily, lying back in the water. "I never got that interview from you. We need to do that soon."

Nathan removed the towel he was wearing and tossed it on the floor. He slid into the tub and took her in his arms.

"Let the interview begin," he said.

Second Chance at Love

WATCH FOR
6 NEW TITLES EVERY MONTH!

Second Chance at Love ™

___ 06148-4	THE STEELE HEART #52 Jocelyn Day	$1.75
___ 06422-X	UNTAMED DESIRE #53 Beth Brookes	$1.75
___ 06651-6	VENUS RISING #54 Michelle Roland	$1.75
___ 06595-1	SWEET VICTORY #55 Jena Hunt	$1.75
___ 06575-7	TOO NEAR THE SUN #56 Aimée Duvall	$1.75
___ 05625-1	MOURNING BRIDE #57 Lucia Curzon	$1.75
___ 06411-4	THE GOLDEN TOUCH #58 Robin James	$1.75
___ 06596-X	EMBRACED BY DESTINY #59 Simone Hadary	$1.75
___ 06660-5	TORN ASUNDER #60 Ann Cristy	$1.75
___ 06573-0	MIRAGE #61 Margie Michaels	$1.75
___ 06650-8	ON WINGS OF MAGIC #62 Susanna Collins	$1.75
___ 05816-5	DOUBLE DECEPTION #63 Amanda Troy	$1.75
___ 06675-3	APOLLO'S DREAM #64 Claire Evans	$1.75
___ 06676-1	SMOLDERING EMBERS #65 Marie Charles	$1.75
___ 06677-X	STORMY PASSAGE #66 Laurel Blake	$1.75
___ 06678-8	HALFWAY THERE #67 Aimée Duvall	$1.75
___ 06679-6	SURPRISE ENDING #68 Elinor Stanton	$1.75
___ 06680-X	THE ROGUE'S LADY #69 Anne Devon	$1.75

WHAT READERS SAY ABOUT
SECOND CHANCE AT LOVE

"SECOND CHANCE AT LOVE is fantastic."
—*J. L., Greenville, South Carolina**

"SECOND CHANCE AT LOVE has all the romance of the big novels."
—*L. W., Oak Grove, Missouri**

"You deserve a standing ovation!"
—*S. C., Birch Run, Michigan**

"Thank you for putting out this type of story. Love and passion have no time limits. I look forward to more of these good books."
—*E. G., Huntsville, Alabama**

"Thank you for your excellent series of books. Our book stores receive their monthly selections between the second and third week of every month. Please believe me when I say they have a frantic female calling them every day until they get your books in."
—*C. Y., Sacramento, California**

"I have become addicted to the SECOND CHANCE AT LOVE books...You can be very proud of these books....I look forward to them each month."
—*D. A., Floral City, Florida**

"I have enjoyed every one of your SECOND CHANCE AT LOVE books. Reading them is like eating potato chips, once you start you just can't stop."
—*L. S., Kenosha, Wisconsin**

"I consider your SECOND CHANCE AT LOVE books the best on the market."
—*D. S., Redmond, Washington**

*Names and addresses available upon request